LADIES AND GENTLEMEN ...

The PENGUINS

By Ivor Davis

Author of *"The Beatles and Me on Tour"*

Illustrations by Dave McTaggart

LADIES AND GENTLEMEN — THE PENGUINS
Cockney Kid Publishing

Illustrations by Dave McTaggart

Copyright © 2018 by Ivor Davis
www.ivordavisbooks.com

Author services by Pedernales Publishing, LLC.
www.pedernalespublishing.com

Library of Congress Control Number: 2018940023

ISBN 978-0-9903710-6-9 Paperback Edition
ISBN 978-0-9903710-5-2 Hardcover Edition
ISBN 978-0-9903710-4-5 Digital Edition

Printed in the United States of America

With *"Ladies and Gentlemen – The Penguins"*
London born, California based **Ivor Davis**,
offers a whimsical tale with Dr. Seussian humor,
about four penguins who dream of being
bigger – well almost – than the most
famous rock band in history: **The Beatles**.

Dave McTaggart is not the Fifth Beatle,
although he was born in Liverpool.
He has illustrated over thirty children's books.

Please allow me to introduce myself

My name is Sadie. I'm a King Penguin and I live in a neat pad in a craggy, windswept shoreline with ocean views in a place called The Falkland Islands - in the middle of the South Atlantic Ocean.

Many of my friends are Gentoo, Macaroni and Magellanic Penguins. And we like to hang out, bask in the sun and swim together in our pool which is right on our front door.

I always wanted to be a rock star - ever since
I stepped out of my egg shell singing...
with a guitar in my flipper.

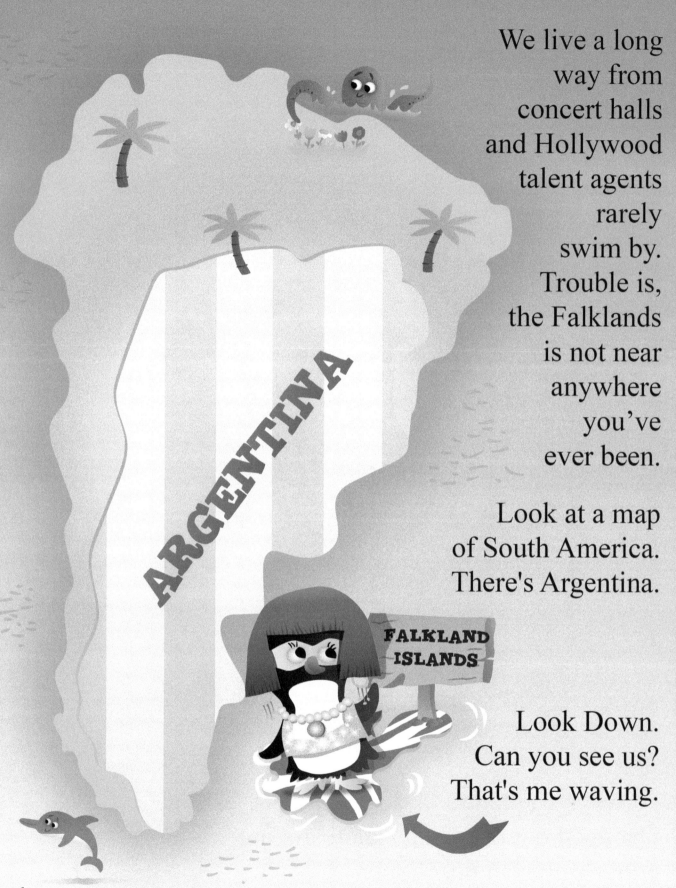

We live a long way from concert halls and Hollywood talent agents rarely swim by. Trouble is, the Falklands is not near anywhere you've ever been.

Look at a map of South America. There's Argentina.

Look Down. Can you see us? That's me waving.

ARGENTINA

FALKLAND ISLANDS

Even though we're only 300 miles from Argentina
we don't speak or sing in Spanish.
But we do dance the tango. **Ole!**

We're very English, living in a British territory.
Every year we celebrate the Queen's birthday.

Even though we are birds we can't fly.
We're great swimmers.
But eight thousand miles to England is a tiring swim.
On the Falklands the population is:
One million penguins.
Half a million sheep who drive us crazy by baaing
all night long.
And two thousand humans.

So there are not many jobs for Penguins
with music in their blood.
So, I decided to form a rock band.
We call ourselves...Guess?
Yes:
The Penguins

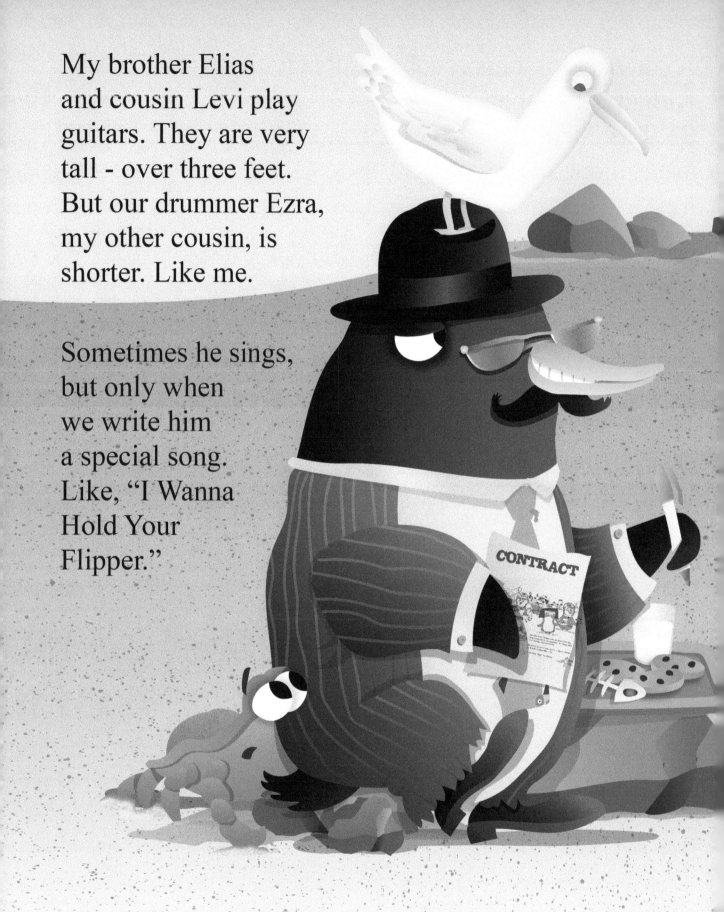

My brother Elias
and cousin Levi play
guitars. They are very
tall - over three feet.
But our drummer Ezra,
my other cousin, is
shorter. Like me.

Sometimes he sings,
but only when
we write him
a special song.
Like, "I Wanna
Hold Your
Flipper."

CONTRACT

One day, Brian Fishstein, who runs the island's
only music store, came to see us perform.
He always wears a suit and tie - even at breakfast.
He said he loved our music and if we signed with him
he would make us bigger than Elvis.

"Yeah. Yeah. Yeah," we all sang.

We're not the only rock group on the Falklands.

There's the Rolling Rockhoppers, who sport fancy plumage and have a big hit, "Hey, Get off of My Island.."

And the Macaroni Plumes with their neat punk haircuts. Their family run a chain of Italian restaurants called *The Macaroni Krill*.

So, we signed with Brian and he got us a gig
on the world famous "Ed Pelican Show."
They loved us.

Suddenly we were hot. We won the international
Crustacean Awards (The Crummies) for our song,
"It's Been a Hard Day's Molting."

The next year we won again for, "We All Live in A Yellow Marine Ecological Reserve."

Penguinmania was everywhere. The Queen gave us the Order of the Penguin Empire (the OPE). We were even bigger than Big Bird.

One day I woke up with a sore beak and feathers falling out.
We were living on room service and salt water from the mini bar.

We loved the crowds. But we missed home and our families. We missed our little paradise.

We missed the homespun joys of dining out at MacSquids or Krillburger.

So we quit. Cold turkey.
Or maybe it should be, cold penguin.

Of course, we're still famous.
And now we get lots of offers to play on cruise ships.

Or write our memoirs.

Which is why I decided to tell you this story.

EVERYTHING YOU WANTED TO KNOW ABOUT PENGUINS BUT WERE AFRAID TO ASK

The Falklands are one of the world's great penguin capitals. As many as a million nest on the islands every summer. And they all look different.
The five species that hang out there are:
Rockhopper, King, Gentoo,
Magellanic and Macaroni.
They are members of the 17 nation penguin family around the world.
Here's how you can avoid offending a Gentoo by calling him a Rockhopper.
Oh, and by the way, their favorite food is Krill.
They're all great swimmers and will go hundreds of miles to feed on oily anchovies.
The oilier the better!

400 pairs of King Penguin
(Aptenodytes patagonicus)

110,000 pairs of Gentoo Penguin (Pygoscelis papua)

50 pairs of Macaroni Penguin (Eudyptes chrysolophus)

130,000 pairs of Magellanic Penguin (Spheniscus magellanicus)

300,000 pairs of Southern Rockhopper Penguin (Eudyptes chrysocome)

FUN FACTS ABOUT THE FALKLANDS:

You'll never stumble across the Falklands by accident.

It's a hard place to find.

Also known, in Spanish, as Islas Malvinas, the Falklands (and there are two – east and west) are a remote South Atlantic archipelago. Don't worry – that big word simply means, "a group of islands stuck in the middle of water."

Visit and you might think you were in the middle of England! It's a British overseas territory, which means most of the 3,000 residents speak with a British accent. It's 8,000 miles from where their Queen lives – in England's Buckingham Palace.

VENEZUELA

COLOMBIA

ECUADOR

PERU

BOLIVIA

DAVID

CHILE

GUYANA

SURINAME

FRENCH
GUIANA

BRAZIL

PARAGUAY

URUGUAY

TRISH

FALKLAND
ISLANDS

ARGENTINA

Since the islands were discovered by seagoing explorers 300 years ago, there's been lots of arguing – even a war – about who really owns the place.

In 1982, Argentina – just 300 miles away – invaded the Falklands. But they were sent home. Today it is peaceful and friendly and still British.

The local *homo sapiens* (it means humans) live alongside half a million sheep and the one million penguins.

No one can tell if the local penguins squawk with a British or Argentinian accent.

A great way to see the Falklands and its capital Stanley, is to visit – as I did – while on a cruise ship.

PENGUIN

One of the most famous music groups in the world are The Beatles, who grew up in Liverpool, England.

Here are their names:

JOHN
(Lennon)

PAUL
(McCartney)

PUZZLE

Take a long look at the illustrations in this book. Now look again. Can YOU be the first to spot their first names?

Clue: All are hiding in the illustrations!

RINGO
(Starr)

GEORGE
(Harrison)

If you want to find out more about the Beatles, go to
www.IvorDavisBeatles.com

COLOR YOUR F

SADIE

ELIAS

27

LEVI

CPSIA information can be obtained
at www.ICGtesting.com
Printed in the USA
LVHW07*1911260618
581976LV00002B/2/P

Black Music Greats

40 inspiring icons

Olivier Cachin & Jérôme Masi

WIDE EYED EDITIONS

From blues to rap

The blues is one of first pages in the history book of popular black American music. Next came rock & roll, and its popularity spread to the world by the 1950s.

Black music, made in America, triggered a chain of transformations: church gospel music transformed into R&B (rhythm and blues), spoken-word poetry became rap. Artists like Sam Cooke and Aretha Franklin grew up from singing between church pews to recording for the biggest American labels. Often, black music reflected political movements and anti-racist liberation struggles. Nina Simone sang of riots in Baltimore, Marvin Gaye, the Vietnam War. During the 1970s, soul singers started singing disco, while funk – a music made to dance to – spread across America via James Brown, George Clinton and others.

Then, the hurricane of hip-hop hit. In 1979, with the track 'Rappers' Delight', the world fell for those word warriors who mixed frenetic rhymes with melodies borrowed from other artists, following the invention of samplers. Rap, the brutal and raw music made by self-taught musicians from the streets, is now the soundtrack to the 21st century.

From Robert Johnson, the mysterious bluesman, to Drake, the rap superstar, through the likes of Stevie Wonder, 2Pac, Whitney Houston and the Fugees, these are the 40 black artists to be listened to and learned about by all.

Contents

21

RUN-DMC

22

ERIC B. & RAKIM

23

PUBLIC ENEMY

24

N.W.A

25

WHITNEY HOUSTON

26

2PAC

27

THE FUGEES

28

SNOOP DOGG

29

THE NOTORIOUS B.I.G.

30

ERYKAH BADU

31

JAY-Z

32

MISSY ELLIOTT

33

KANYE WEST

34

BEYONCÉ

35

PHARRELL
WILLIAMS

36

RIHANNA

37

LIL WAYNE

38

DRAKE

39

NICKI MINAJ

40

THE WEEKND

Robert Johnson

Robert Johnson is known as the father of blues. The blues was a musical genre born in the Mississippi Delta, with its roots in African music and African American work songs. A genius on the guitar, the legend goes that Johnson sold his soul to the devil to achieve musical success. He died when he was just 27, and he only ever recorded 29 songs, which were still enough to see him influence the greats, including Keith Richards of the Rolling Stones and Eric Clapton, who called Johnson 'the most important blues singer that ever lived'.

SCANDAL

The cause of Johnson's death remains a mystery, but it is thought he may have been poisoned.

GREATEST HIT

Of all Johnson's recordings, the most famous of his songs is 'Me and the Devil Blues', which tells the story of him selling his soul to the devil.

THREE DATES

1933
Meets bluesman Johnny Shines.

23 NOVEMBER 1936
Records his first songs in a hotel room.

16 AUGUST 1938
Dies aged 27, near Greenwood, Mississippi.

GUITAR GOD

Seventy years after Johnson's death, *Rolling Stone* magazine placed him at number 5 in its list of the 100 greatest guitarists of all time. *Spin*, another American publication, gave him top spot in their list of guitar gods.

RECOGNITION

Forgotten for many years, Johnson was rediscovered by professional guitarists who admired his work. He was inaugurated into the first edition of the Rock & Roll Hall of Fame, in 1986, in recognition of his influence on the birth of rock.

DANDY

Johnson wore a hat, three-piece suit and a cravat.

DEVILISH

He was said to have the brazen look of a blues singer who had signed a deal with the devil.

MUSICAL STYLE
Delta blues, blues

KEY DATES
Born in 1911, died in 1938

GUITAR

Johnson's instrument of choice was an acoustic guitar.

The master of the blues

Nina Simone

THREE DATES

1964
Records first album, *Nina Simone in Concert*, at New York's Carnegie Hall.

1992
Publishes her autobiography, *I Put a Spell on You*, written while in Amsterdam.

21 APRIL 2003
Dies at home in her sleep.

Born Eunice Kathleen Waymon, she would eventually change her name to Nina Simone to stop her family members realising she was a musician. She grew up in a poor family in North Carolina. She learned to play the piano at the age of three but wasn't allowed into music school because of her black skin. Simone then dedicated her career to anti-racist music. From classical to blues, Simone's enchanting voice has influenced many artists, including Elton John, who has named one of his pianos after her.

INFLUENCES

Simone sought inspiration in the songs of Billie Holiday, who like her, battled both racism and illness.

A BAD DEAL

Simone's 1958 song 'I Loves You, Porgy' was a huge hit. Unfortunately she sold the rights for $3,000 and the record company made millions of dollars.

A NEW NAME

Her choice of stage name blended her childhood nickname 'Nina' from *niña*, which means 'girl' in Spanish, with the first name of Simone Signoret, who was her favourite French actress.

SCANDAL

In 1995, struggling with her mental health, Simone injured her neighbour's son, because he was disturbing her from her work.

2

MUSICAL STYLE
Soul, blues, gospel, jazz, classical music

KEY DATES
Born in 1933, died in 2003

BLACK POWER

Simone wore her hair in an afro, typical of 1970s Black Power activists.

PRIDE

Simone embodied the pride of a black woman battling prejudice.

AFRICAN

Her large beaded necklaces recalled her African heritage.

The high priestess of soul

James Brown

James Brown led a dramatic life. He was born into a poor family and as a teenager he spent three years in prison , where he learned to play the guitar and piano. He started his career as part of the group the Famous Flames. He was a famously bossy lead singer and fined the other musicians if they played a wrong note. He is credited with inventing funk, which is a more rhythmic style of R&B, with his dance hits 'Papa's Got a Brand New Bag' and 'Say It Loud (I'm Black and I'm Proud)', which became the Black Power anthem of the 1970s.

ON THE BIG SCREEN

Brown's story was recounted in the film *Get On Up* (2014). Chadwick Boseman plays Brown, but the film uses the original versions of 'It's a Man's Man's Man's World' and 'Papa's Got a Brand New Bag' sung by James Brown himself.

THREE DATES

5 APRIL 1968
Performs in Boston the day after the assassination of Martin Luther King.

20 JUNE 1980
Stars in John Landis's film *The Blues Brothers*.

1988
Releases *I'm Real*, an album produced by hip-hop group Full Force.

BESTSELLER

'Get Up', released in 1970, reached second place in the R&B charts and was the first hit by his new group, the J.B.'s.

RAPPER'S DELIGHT

Brown's music has been sampled by thousands of hip-hop artists, and his powerful rhythms have featured on tracks by Public Enemy and De La Soul. He even appears in MC Hammer's music video for 'Too Legit to Quit'.

3

FUNKY

This 'Soul Brother Number One' always wore funky, eccentric sunglasses.

MUSICAL STYLE
Funk, soul, disco, R&B, hip-hop

KEY DATES
Born in 1933, died in 2006

GOS

James Brown is often called the Godfather of Soul and he had these initials on his belt.

PINT-SIZED PRINCE

Brown was on the shorter side, and wore Cuban heels to give him a bit of extra height.

GOS

The godfather of soul

Sly & The Family Stone

Sly Stone founded his group, the Family Stone, in San Francisco in 1966. The band included men and women who were both black and white – a real revolution at the time! The group's music was also mixed, blending psychedelic rock with funk and soul. However, Sly's musical genius was blighted by drug addiction, and concerts were often cancelled. Although Sly hasn't released an album since 1982 or toured since 2007, his influence is everlasting and he is admired by Stevie Wonder, OutKast and Prince.

BESTSELLER

Stand!, released in 1969, is the group's classic album, featuring their first number one, 'Everyday People', and 'I Want to Take You Higher'.

THREE DATES

17 AUGUST 1969
Perform an explosive concert at Woodstock.

20 NOVEMBER 1971
Release the album *There's a Riot Goin' On* with the American flag on its cover.

17 JULY 1974
Sly Stone goes on live TV across America with the boxer Muhammad Ali.

ADMIRED

Sly was loved by Michael Jackson, who admired the band's ability to transcend race and musical genre. Jackson purchased their entire catalogue of music, of which 'Family Affair' and 'Thank You (Falettinme Be Mice Elf Agin)' are the most famous.

CONTROVERSY

In 1969, Sly fought with the Black Panther party, who were demanding that he fire his white manager and bandmates. Sly refused and hired gangsters to act as body guards in order to protect himself.

4

MUSICAL STYLE
Psychedelic rock, soul, funk

KEY DATES
Sylvester Stewart, AKA Sly Stone, born in 1943

'FLOWER POWER'

Their beaded necklaces showed their hippie roots.

DIVERSE

Black and white, men and women, they were the first diverse musical group to hit the big time in the 1960s.

PSYCHEDELIC LOOK

The band members wore wild clothes in bright colours.

The mixed, multiracial mega-group

Miles Davis

A genius on the trumpet, Miles Davis blew traditional jazz wide open. After he first appeared in Charlie Parker's group, Davis went on to make musical history. His album *Birth of the Cool* was released in 1957 and was the beginning of 'West Coast jazz'. Miles Davis was influenced by other musical genres, and mixed jazz with funk, and even rap for his final album. This helped him to stay at the forefront of the developments in jazz throughout his career, which lasted over 50 years.

MUTED SOUND

Miles Davis played the trumpet with a plug in the end called a mute. This gave it a different sound. It became his signature sound and it influenced jazz to come.

CULT ALBUM

Kind of Blue is one of the greatest jazz albums ever recorded and is Davis's bestseller, with more than four million copies sold.

POSTHUMOUS

For his final album *Doo-Bop*, released in 1992, Davis wanted to collaborate with rap musicians. In the end, his producer Easy Mo Bee had to finish the album without Davis, for only six songs had been finished before his death.

CONCERT

In July 1991, Davis played in Paris as part of a super group with Herbie Hancock, Wayne Shorter, Chick Corea, Bill Evans and Joe Zawinul.

SELECTED DISCOGRAPHY

1952
Young Man with a Horn

1959
Kind of Blue

1972
On the Corner

5

DETERMINATION

Davis possessed the glare of a musician who was completely dedicated to his art.

INSTRUMENT

Davis was never without his gleaming trumpet.

MUSIC FIRST

'Good music is good no matter what kind of music it is.'

MUSICAL STYLE
Jazz

KEY DATES
Born in 1926, died in 1991

The jazz revolutionary

Diana Ross & The Supremes

Diana Ernestine Earle Ross was born and raised in Detroit. Detroit was home to Motown Records and Ross would become one of their biggest stars. Ross' group was called The Supremes and they were famous for dressing in sumptuous silks and glittering gowns, and showing the luxurious side of soul. Ross also acted and played Dorothy in *The Wiz*, which was a rewriting of *The Wizard of Oz*. Many musicians since have been inspired by Ross, including Mariah Carey, Beyoncé and Taylor Swift!

Ross had many hits, but 'Muscles' is unforgettable. Written for Ross by Michael Jackson, 'Muscles' was the name of Jackson's pet snake.

SELECTED DISCOGRAPHY

AS A GROUP

1964
Where Did Our Love Go

1966
The Supremes A' Go-Go

AS A SOLO ARTIST

1979
The Boss

2006
Blue

GOSPEL

It was in the pews of her Baptist church that Ross first learned to sing, much like Aretha Franklin and many other black American artists. Ross's grandfather, William, was a pastor in Alabama.

SOUL SAMPLING

Ross's work was brought to a whole new audience when famous rappers sampled her songs. Notorious B.I.G. and producer P. Diddy used 'I'm Coming Out' for their hit 'Mo Money Mo Problems'. 'You Can't Hurry Love' was used by Phil Collins in 1983.

Ross's comeback album *Diana* featured the disco classic 'Upside Down'.

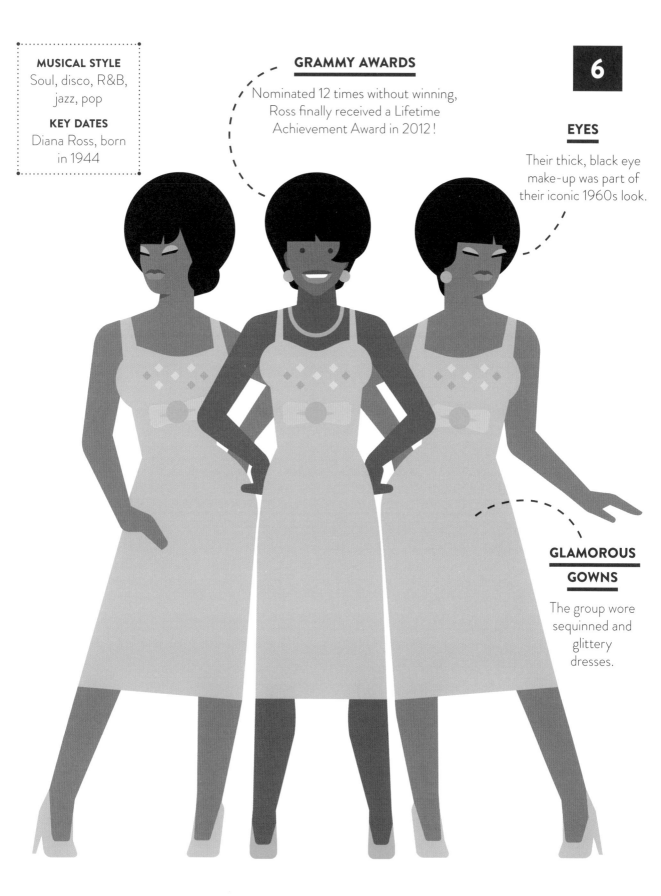

MUSICAL STYLE
Soul, disco, R&B, jazz, pop

KEY DATES
Diana Ross, born in 1944

GRAMMY AWARDS
Nominated 12 times without winning, Ross finally received a Lifetime Achievement Award in 2012!

6

EYES
Their thick, black eye make-up was part of their iconic 1960s look.

GLAMOROUS GOWNS
The group wore sequinned and glittery dresses.

The queens of Motown

The Jackson 5

For five years, the five Jackson brothers made up the most popular group in the United States. Michael was the youngest but the biggest star. They were managed by Berry Gordy, who was head of the Motown record label. The Jacksons invented a pop version of soul called 'bubble-gum soul'. Their first singles, 'ABC', 'I Want You Back', 'The Love You Save' and 'I'll Be There', were all top of the charts. In 1975 they changed their name to just The Jacksons. Michael launched a solo career and became the King of Pop.

CULT ALBUM

Diana Ross Presents The Jackson 5 launched in 1969. The group covered soul classics and *Zip-a-Dee-Doo-Dah*, a song from the film *Song of the South*.

INFLUENCES

The brothers were inspired by Diana Ross, who was the star singer of the Supremes. She became their godmother while they were all signed to Motown.

AUDITION

To be signed to Motown, the five brothers had to pass an audition in which they sung, danced and played instruments. At the time Michael was just 11, but Motown made him pretend to be 9 so that people would be even more amazed by his talent.

JACKSONMANIA

The sudden and enormous success of the group led to a phenomenon called 'Jackson-mania'. They were so popular in America that a TV cartoon series was made, with the bro-thers as the main characters.

SELECTED DISCOGRAPHY

1970
ABC

1971
Goin' Back to Indiana

1973
The Jackson 5 in Japan

1974
Dancing Machine

1975
Moving Violation

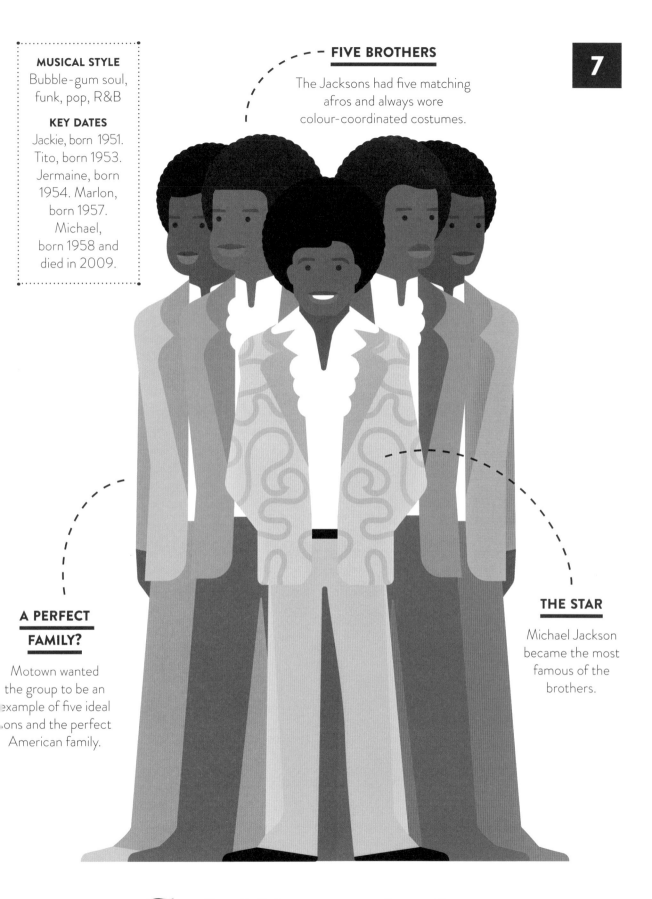

7

MUSICAL STYLE
Bubble-gum soul, funk, pop, R&B

KEY DATES
Jackie, born 1951. Tito, born 1953. Jermaine, born 1954. Marlon, born 1957. Michael, born 1958 and died in 2009.

FIVE BROTHERS
The Jacksons had five matching afros and always wore colour-coordinated costumes.

A PERFECT FAMILY?
Motown wanted the group to be an example of five ideal sons and the perfect American family.

THE STAR
Michael Jackson became the most famous of the brothers.

The bubble-gum brothers

Marvin Gaye

Marvin Gaye was a singer, writer and drummer, and he defined the sound of soul at Motown Records. Gaye started singing in church at the age of four. His first single, 'Let Your Conscience Be Your Guide', came out in 1961. Gaye sang about love, but he also touched on more adult themes. In the album *What's Going On*, he sang about drugs, poverty and the Vietnam War. The album was initially rejected but became one of Marvin Gaye's biggest successes, containing some of his most recognisable songs.

SCANDAL
During a family argument, Gaye was shot and killed by his own father, Marvin Gay Senior.

GREATEST HIT
In 1968, Marvin Gaye had his first number one hit with 'I Heard It Through the Grapevine'.

EMOTION AND TECHNIQUE

With a singing range of four octaves, Gaye could go from a deep baritone to a high tenor in the same breath. His perfect technique was paired with raw emotion, as heard in the song 'Pride and Joy'.

SOULFUL SEPARATION

While going through a difficult divorce, Gaye recorded *Here, My Dear*, a regretful and honest record that tells of a couple's struggle. All the profits from the album went to his ex-wife Anna.

SELECTED DISCOGRAPHY

1962
That Stubborn Kinda' Fellow

1968
I Heard It Through the Grapevine

1971
What's Going On

1973
Let's Get It On

1982
Midnight Love

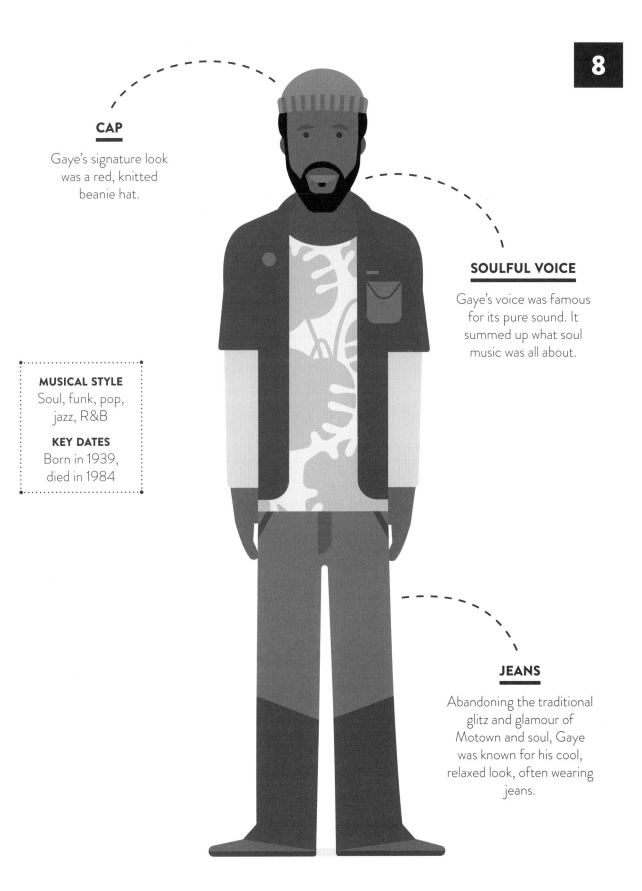

8

CAP

Gaye's signature look was a red, knitted beanie hat.

SOULFUL VOICE

Gaye's voice was famous for its pure sound. It summed up what soul music was all about.

MUSICAL STYLE
Soul, funk, pop, jazz, R&B

KEY DATES
Born in 1939, died in 1984

JEANS

Abandoning the traditional glitz and glamour of Motown and soul, Gaye was known for his cool, relaxed look, often wearing jeans.

The golden voice of soul

Stevie Wonder

Born blind as a result of his premature birth, Stevie Wonder became the child prodigy of Motown, baptised 'Little Stevie Wonder, the 12 Year Old Genius'. Once an adult, Wonder recorded innovative but popular albums, and he dominated the charts with hits like 'Fingertips', 'Happy Birthday' and 'Sir Duke'. His song 'Village Ghetto Land' highlights Wonder's commitment to black liberation. An outstanding piano player, he is one of the most respected personalities in music.

CONCERT

In October 1975, in Kingston, Jamaica, Bob Marley accompanied Wonder to perform 'I Shot the Sheriff' and 'Superstition'.

SELECTED DISCOGRAPHY

1962
The Jazz Soul of Little Stevie

1969
My Cherie Amour

1972
Music of My Mind

1980
Hotter Than July

2004
A Time to Love

MOTOWN STORY

Motown Records, created by Berry Gordy at the end of the 1950s, brought soul music to the public. With the Jackson 5, The Temptations, The Four Tops and Marvin Gaye, Motown made waves.

STEVIE & PRINCE

In July 2010, in Bercy in Paris, Prince entered the stage during one of Stevie Wonder's concerts to sing a duet version of 'Superstition'. The crowd, understandably, went wild.

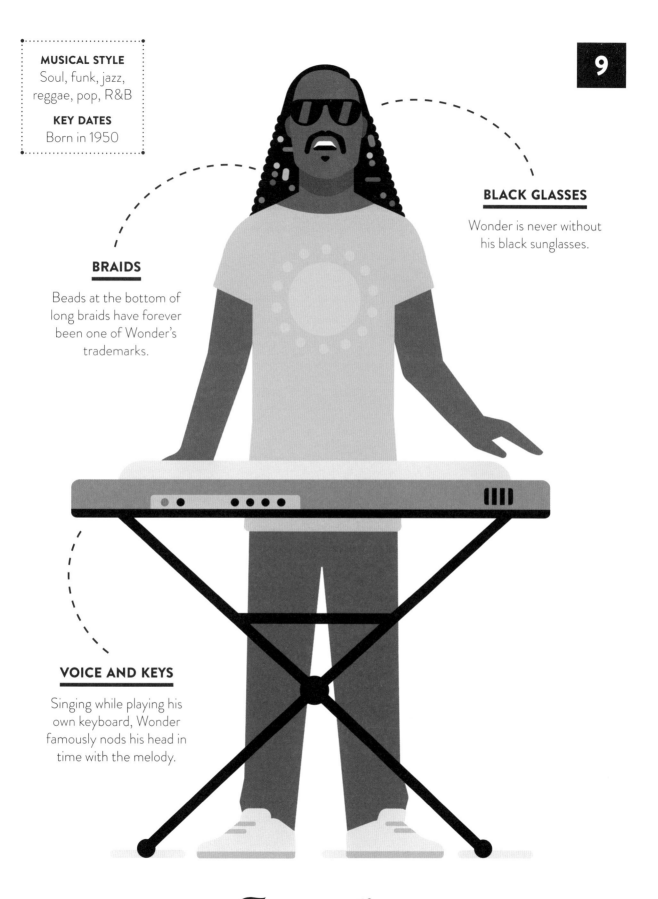

9

MUSICAL STYLE
Soul, funk, jazz, reggae, pop, R&B

KEY DATES
Born in 1950

BLACK GLASSES
Wonder is never without his black sunglasses.

BRAIDS
Beads at the bottom of long braids have forever been one of Wonder's trademarks.

VOICE AND KEYS
Singing while playing his own keyboard, Wonder famously nods his head in time with the melody.

The prodigy

Aretha Franklin

Aretha Franklin was the daughter of a travelling Catholic preacher and loved singing in church, before she got a record deal. She joined Atlantic Records in 1967, where her career took flight thanks to her powerful voice and R&B style. Franklin's biggest hits include 'I Say a Little Prayer', 'Respect' and 'Natural Woman'. She has also sung duets with younger female musicians like Whitney Houston and Lauryn Hill. In 1986, Franklin was the first woman to enter the Rock & Roll Hall of Fame.

GREATEST HIT

'Respect', from 1967, was one of Franklin's first classics. Originally a ballad, it was rearranged to be more funky and became a hit.

SOUL FAMILY

As a close friend of Cissy Houston, Franklin would bounce Cissy's daughter Whitney Houston upon her knee. As a child, Whitney called Aretha 'Auntie Ree', as an adult she would record music with Franklin.

CONCERT

In 2009, Franklin sang 'My Country 'Tis of Thee' at the White House for the inauguration of Barack Obama, the first black American President.

POP, SOUL, DISCO

For her last studio album, *Aretha Franklin Sings the Great Diva Classics*, Franklin pays homage to the classics of pop, soul and disco: 'Rolling in the Deep' by Adele, 'I Will Survive' by Gloria Gaynor, and 'Nothing Compares 2 U' by Sinéad O'Connor.

SELECTED DISCOGRAPHY

1968
Lady Soul

1971
Aretha Live At Fillmore West

1979
La Diva

10

MUSICAL STYLE
Soul, gospel, jazz, disco, pop, R&B

KEY DATES
Born in 1942, died in 2018

DAUGHTER OF A PREACHER MAN

Franklin drew on her experience as a church singer, which has led to her music being called 'gospel-charged soul'.

MAGIC VOICE

Her powerful, heart-rending voice works perfectly in emotional soul ballads.

CLASSY STYLE

Franklin's wardrobe changed from that of a humble church mouse to a soul diva.

From gospel to R&B

Earth, Wind & Fire

Maurice White founded Earth, Wind & Fire in Chicago in 1970. First of all they played a danced-up version of jazz but later became known for disco funk. They were passionate about Egyptology, which inspired a lot of their songs and the images on their album covers. They hit the big time with tracks like 'Let's Groove', 'Fantasy' and 'September'. Maurice sang tenor and played the kalimba, an African thumb piano, while Philip Bailey was the soulful singer with a distinctive high-pitched, falsetto, voice.

CONCERT

In January 1979, EW&F played a concert for Music for UNICEF, appearing alongside Donna Summer and the Bee Gees.

FUNKY MAGIC

At their most successful, the group would put together elaborate shows on stages shaped like Egyptian pyramids and with world-famous magicians performing alongside them.

PARKINSON'S

Maurice White stopped touring with the band in 1994 when he became very ill with Parkinson's disease. He died in Los Angeles on 4 February 2016, aged 74.

BESTSELLER

In 1979, their album *I Am* went double platinum, which meant it sold over two million copies. This was thanks to the success of tracks 'Boogie Wonderland' and 'After the Love Has Gone'.

11

MUSICAL STYLE
Funk, soul, disco, electro, jazz, rock, pop

MEMBERS
Maurice White, Philip Bailey, Verdine White, Al McKay, Ralph Johnson

COSTUMES
The group wore super-funky outfits that were sometimes decorated with symbols from Egyptology.

PRESIDENTIAL PICK
In March 2000, EW&F played at the White House for Bill Clinton and his guest, the King of Morocco, Mohammed VI.

BROTHERHOOD
Maurice White's brother Verdine White also played in the band as a bassist.

Disco funk with an Egyptian twist

Isaac Hayes

CONCERT

On 20 August 1972, at the Los Angeles Memorial Coliseum, Hayes performed at the Wattstax festival in front of a crowd of 10,000 people.

Isaac Hayes was a giant of soul. He was signed to the record label Stax as a writer, producer and session musician which means that he played instruments on other people's songs. His solo albums showed off his distinctive, deep voice and his ear for musical arrangement. Hayes was the third back person ever to have won an Oscar, which was for his soundtrack to the film *Shaft*. He was also a talented film actor and the voice of Chef in the animated series *South Park*.

BLACKSPLOITATION

During the 1970s, American cinema produced a genre of films in which the heroes and heroines were black. In 1974, Isaac acted with Lino Ventura in *Tough Guys*, for which he also composed the soundtrack.

SELECTED DISCOGRAPHY

1969
Hot Buttered Soul

1970
The Isaac Hayes Movement

1971
Black Moses

1975
Disco Connection

1995
Branded

SCANDAL

In March 2006 Hayes left his role in *South Park* after eight years because of an episode that mocked the Scientology religion.

THE LONG GAME

Skilled at writing very long songs, Hayes's 13-minute version of 'By the Time I Get to Phoenix' begins with him speaking and is considered one of his classics.

LOOK

Hayes had an iconic and spectacular look. He loved to perform without a shirt.

12

ISAAC AND RAP

'It feels so good to have influenced rap – it gives me a sense of longevity'.

GOLD CHAINS

Hayes wore big gold chains long before rappers made them their favourite accessory.

MUSICAL STYLE
Soul, funk, disco, R&B

KEY DATES
Born in 1942, died in 2008

The black Moses

Tina Turner

Tina Turner was born in the south of America in Tennessee. She started her music career singing in Ike Turner's (her husband) R&B group. They started recording under the name Ike & Tina Turner, but later separated in 1973 as a result of Ike's drug-taking and violence. Tina took a break from music for a while but returned in the 1980s with a new mature sound and released popular hits like 'What's Love Got to Do with It?' She is known as 'the queen of rock and roll'.

FIVE DATES

1957
Meets Ike Turner.

1966
Releases *River Deep Mountain High*, produced by Phil Spector.

1984
Worldwide acclaim for album *Private Dancer*

1985
Cast in the film *Mad Max Beyond Thunderdome*.

1995
Sings the title credit theme for James Bond, *GoldenEye*, written by U2.

CONCERT

In 1985, Tina participated in the enormous charity concert Live Aid, where she sang 'It's Only Rock 'n Roll' as a duet with Mick Jagger.

ACID QUEEN

In 1974, Turner performed in *Tommy*, a rock opera written by British band The Who. She played the terrible Acid Queen, a troubled, modern-day witch. The following year Turner released *Acid Queen*, a solo album.

THE PAY-OFF PAID OFF

The producer Phil Spector paid Turner's ex husband, Ike, $20,000 to stay out of the way while they recorded the song 'River Deep Mountain High'. Spector said it is one of the best songs he has ever produced, so it must have been worth it!

13

MANE

Tina Turner's hair is instantly recognisable. It has amazing volume, like a lion's mane.

MUSICAL STYLE
Rock, pop, R&B, dance, soul

KEY DATES
Born Anna Mae Bullock in 1939

WITH BOWIE

She is as talented at singing rock music as she is at soul. She has sung with rock greats, including David Bowie.

HIGH ENERGY

Turner is a ball of energy when she performs. She doesn't dance on stage but her stage presence is explosive.

The queen of rock & roll

Donna Summer

It was while performing in the comedy musical *Hair* in Germany that Donna Summer met producer Giorgio Moroder, who asked her to sing 'Love to Love You Baby' in 1975. The reign of disco was under way, and Donna became the queen. She had 14 top-ten hits in nine years. Summer achieved a lot during her life. She worked for the charity UNICEF, won an Oscar for her song 'Last Dance' and is ranked the sixth most successful dance artist of all time. In 2012 she died in Florida after battling lung cancer.

CULT ALBUM

The soundtrack to *Thank God It's Friday* features three of Summer's disco funk songs, among others by the Commodores and Diana Ross.

GREATEST HIT

The song 'I Feel Love', produced in 1977 by Giorgio Moroder, has inspired generations of DJs. David Bowie said it was the 'sound of the future'.

SELECTED DISCOGRAPHY

1976
A Love Trilogy

1977
I Remember Yesterday

1979
Bad Girls

1983
She Works Hard for the Money

2008
Crayons

HOMOPHOBIA

During the mid-1980s, the singer, who had become very religious, made homophobic remarks and her work was then boycotted by the gay community. Summer later apologised, saying that she had been misunderstood.

MUSICAL

In 1978, Summer played a lead role in the film *Thank God It's Friday*, a disco music comedy. In it she played Nicole Sims, an aspiring singer.

14

MUSICAL STYLE
Disco, pop, rock, soul, electro

KEY DATES
Born in 1948, died in 2012

DANCE MUSIC

Her song 'I Feel Love' marked the beginning of dance music.

STYLE ICON

Summer's 1970s dresses were chic and typical of the disco era.

POWER MOVE

Summer's powerful poses when she performed cemented her position as the first true disco diva.

The original disco diva

Bob Marley & the Wailers

Robert Nesta Marley was born in Jamaica where he met the producer Lee 'Scratch' Perry. Together they would record Bob Marley's first huge hits. From 1974 Marley's career took off, and the reggae roots he played with his band, the Wailers, captivated the entire world. The group included Peter Tosh and Bunny Wailer. Together they released historic hit albums. Marley died from skin cancer at only 36, having spread the music of his homeland across the whole planet.

ATTACK

In December 1976, two days before the Smile Jamaica concert, unknown gunmen attacked Marley at his home. Despite his injuries, Marley still performed, accompanied by a brass band.

SELECTED DISCOGRAPHY

1973
Catch a Fire

1977
Exodus

1978
Kaya

1979
Survival

ROOTS, PUNK, REGGAE

In 1977, having just released the album *Exodus*, Marley loved the British punk so much that he recorded 'Punky Reggae Party' with Lee Perry, in which he references The Clash, The Damned and The Jam.

GREATEST HIT

'No Woman No Cry' is the most famous Bob Marley song: it has been covered hundreds of times in every musical style.

CONCERT

When Zimbabwe became independent in 1980, Bob Marley paid for his own ticket to go and play at the celebrations.

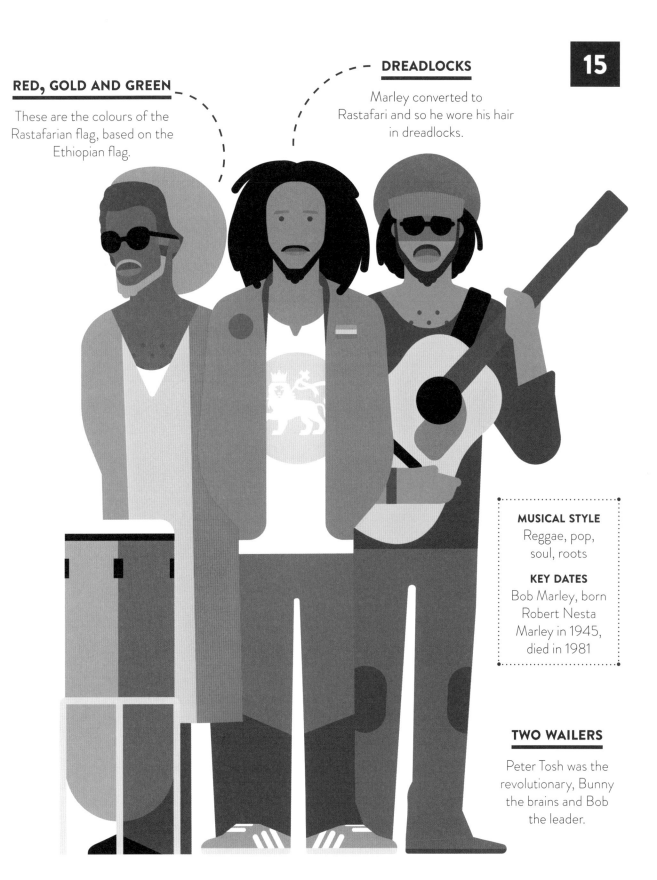

15

RED, GOLD AND GREEN

These are the colours of the Rastafarian flag, based on the Ethiopian flag.

DREADLOCKS

Marley converted to Rastafari and so he wore his hair in dreadlocks.

MUSICAL STYLE
Reggae, pop, soul, roots

KEY DATES
Bob Marley, born Robert Nesta Marley in 1945, died in 1981

TWO WAILERS

Peter Tosh was the revolutionary, Bunny the brains and Bob the leader.

The reggae superstars

Prince

Born in the same year as Madonna and Michael Jackson, Prince Rogers Nelson signed his first record deal at the age of 19. Prince was a virtuoso and played all the instrumental parts on his first album *For You*. On later albums he enlisted a band called The Revolution. Prince's 1984 hit-filled album, *Purple Rain*, catapulted him to fame and he played the lead role in the film of the same name. Prince travelled the world on tour, giving performances that lasted up to three hours! He died after accidentally taking too many pain killers.

SCANDAL

In 1987, Prince announced the release of the *Black Album*, but changed his mind after he thought the lyrics were 'too negative'. The album was only released in 1994.

FOUR DATES

1984
Releases 'Purple Rain', which tops the charts for 24 weeks in a row.

1989
Writes the music for Tim Burton's *Batman*.

1989
Changes his name to the unpronounceable symbol: ⚥

1996
Releases a triple CD called *Emancipation*, featuring 36 tracks.

CONCERT

All of Prince's shows are the stuff of legend, but his October 2009 performance at La Cigale in Paris lasted three hours with six encores!

NUMEROUS NAMES

Prince loved to sign his many and diverse projects using different names. He has been credited with the names Christopher, Camille, Jamie Starr, The Artist, ⚥, and even, The Artist Formerly Known as Prince.

PAISLEY PARK

Prince founded the record label Paisley Park in 1985. His recording studio has the same name. At his recording studio there is a locked vault filled with music that Prince made before he died but that no one has ever heard before.

16

DANCE MACHINE

Prince was an outstanding dancer, who loved to do the splits on stage, just like James Brown!

STAR GUITAR

Prince's custom-made guitar was in the shape of his own logo, ♀, a mash-up of the symbols for man and woman.

MUSICAL STYLE
Funk, rock, soul, R&B, pop, house, folk

KEY DATES
Born Prince Rogers Nelson in 1958, died in 2016

COLOURFUL SUITS

Prince loved to dress in flamboyant colours, especially purple, orange and black.

The purple priest of pop

Fela Kuti

Born in Nigeria to a reverend father and a feminist activist mother, Fela Anikulapo Kuti was the champion of afrobeat. Afrobeat is a hypnotic rythmic genre of music that Fela developed over his 50 albums. He wrote long, mesmerising songs that sometimes lasted 30 minutes. Fela also founded Afrika Shrine, a concert hall in the centre of Lagos, the capital of Nigeria. Forever at war with the government, Fela was imprisoned numerous times. After he died, his son Femi continued to make afrobeat like his dad.

SCANDAL

When Fela was diagnosed with AIDS he refused treatment. His funeral saw a million Nigerians march in procession.

CULT ALBUM

Released in 1979, 'International Thief Thief' attacked then Nigerian president Obasanjo and the communications company ITT, who financed political coups worldwide.

SAX-MANIAC

Fela's favourite instrument was the saxophone, but he also loved the piano, the trumpet and the guitar. His drummer, Tony Allen, a pioneer of afrobeat, played alongside Fela for 20 years.

ON STAGE

In 2009, the American musical show called *Fela!* opened on Broadway. This musical was based on Fela's vast musical catalogue, and was financed by lots of musicians, including Jay-Z and Will Smith.

SELECTED DISCOGRAPHY

1971
Why Black Man Dey Suffer

1976
Zombie

1977
Sorrow, Tears and Blood

1980
Coffin for Head of State

1985
Army Arrangement

17

ACTIVIST

Fela said that 'Music is the weapon of the future'.

MUSICAL STYLE
Afrobeat, Ghanaian Highlife, funk, jazz

KEY DATES
Born in 1938, died in 1997

SAXOPHONE

The tenor saxophone was his favourite instrument.

MODERN TRIBAL

Bare-chested with tribal face paint, Fela played avant-garde music that linked Africa's rich heritage to the future.

The master of afrobeat

The Last Poets

At the end of the 1960s, several young activists affiliated with the Black Panthers met in a New York warehouse to write poetry and make music together. They called themselves the Last Poets and their controversial work saw them targeted by the CIA. Along with their close friend, the musician Gil Scott-Heron, they are seen as the 'grandfathers of rap'. Over time, the Poets' music developed, and their work is not only known as the starting point of rap but the only group in the genre 'jazzoetry' (jazz and poetry).

SCANDAL

In 1970, their song 'The Pill', which criticised the contraceptive pill, sparked huge debate.

SELECTED DISCOGRAPHY

1971
This Is Madness

1976
Delights of the Garden

1984
Oh My People

1993
Holy Terror

1994
Scatterap/Home

JALAL THE REBEL

In 1973, the leader of the Poets, Jalal, wrote *Hustlers Convention*, one of the very first rap albums, under the pseudonym Lightnin' Rod. The album featured Kool & The Gang, as well as jazz musicians like Cornell Dupree and Eric Gale.

POETRY AND RAP

Umar Bin Hassan, one of the founding members of the Last Poets, was invited by the rapper Common to perform on the track 'The Corner', produced by Kanye West in 2005.

18

MUSICAL STYLE
Poetry, jazz, rap, funk, electro

KEY DATES
Abiodun Oyewole born in 1948
Umar Bin Hassan born in 1948,
Jalal Nuriddin born in 1944,
died in 2018

PIONEERS
Speaking about rap today: 'We remember when these rappers were still in diapers' – Jalal

AFRICAN TUNICS
The group wore African clothing before it became fashionable among some rappers in the 1980s.

DJEMBES
African drums formed the backbone of the group's first albums.

The grandfathers of rap

Chic

The guitarist Nile Rodgers and bassist Bernard Edwards were the backbone of Chic, which is known as the greatest disco group of the 1980s and 1990s. With sumptuous arrangements, featuring violins and orchestras played by master musicians, they wrote hit after hit: 'Everybody Dance', 'Le Freak' and 'Stage Fright'. They also produced albums for Blondie, Sister Sledge and the rock band Duran Duran. After the death of Edwards, Rodgers has continued to play as Chic, with their latest song released in 2015.

COUNTERATTACK

Furious at having been refused entry to the prestigious nightclub Studio 54, Nile and Bernard composed 'Le Freak', which became a huge success.

CONCERT

In April 1996, Chic played the Budokan in Tokyo with Slash and Sister Sledge as guests. Bernard Edwards would die the following day.

ECLECTIC

Nile Rodgers is a prolific and eclectic producer, who has worked with Diana Ross, David Bowie (*Let's Dance*), Madonna (*Like a Virgin*), Mick Jagger, Michael Jackson, Eric Clapton and Duran Duran.

GREATEST HIT

'Good Times', released in 1978, is Chic's classic track: it encompasses the pure nostalgia and spirit of disco.

FIVE DATES

1970
Rodgers and Edwards launch their first band, The Boys.

1978
Produce *We Are Family* for Sister Sledge.

1983
Nile Rodgers produces *Let's Dance* for Bowie.

1984
Group splits for the first time.

2003
Tony Thompson, the band's drummer, dies.

19

SUITS

The group dressed suavely in suits like businessmen. In short, they were chic!

SUNGLASSES

Their sophisticated sunnies were elegant and discreet.

ROCK ATTITUDE

'We are the rock band for the disco movement.'

MUSICAL STYLE
Disco, soul, funk, rock, R&B

KEY DATES
Nile Rodgers, born in 1952. Bernard Edwards, born in 1952, died in 1996

Disco royalty

The Sugarhill Gang

The Sugarhill Gang were a trio that included Wonder Mike, Master Gee and Big Bank Hank. In 1979 they released the song 'Rapper's Delight' which took hip-hop straight to the top of the charts for the first time. Produced by Sylvia Robinson, a soul singer with her own label, the 15-minute-long track samples Chic's song 'Good Times'. After their smash hit, the Gang's career was less celebrated, but still impressive: they collaborated with electronic DJ Bob Sinclar in 2009 to create 'La La Song'.

GREATEST HIT

The Gang never surpassed the success of their biggest track 'Rapper's Delight', which was a hit all over the world and launched American rap.

CASTING

The producer Sylvia Robinson selected the three rappers who made up the Gang, like they were in a boy band. She had actually met Big Bank Hank in a restaurant, where he was making pizzas.

RENAISSANCE

In 2016, the Sugarhill Gang reformed for a worldwide tour, with Henry 'Hen Dogg' Williams replacing Hank. They could even use the original band name, which has always been the property of the group's producer Sylvia Robinson.

INFLUENCES

The Sugarhill Gang represent old-school rap and remain a constant reference for the younger generation of rap artists.

20

MUSICAL STYLE
Old-school rap

KEY DATES
Master Gee, born Guy O'Brien in 1963.
Wonder Mike, born Michael Wright in 1958.
Big Bank Hank, born Henry Lee Jackson in 1956 and died in 2014.

'RAPPER'S DELIGHT'

'I said a hip, hop, the hippie, the hippie to the hip hip-hop...'
(intro to 'Rappers' Delight').

MELODIC RAP

The Gang's style was heavily influenced by funk and disco.

VINTAGE
The Gang's retro look was flashy and funky.

Old-school cool

Run-DMC

Founded in the New York suburb of Queens, the trio Run-DMC was made up of two rappers (Joseph Simmons, aka Run, and Darryl McDaniels, aka DMC) and one DJ (Jason Mizell, aka Jam Master Jay). Their sharp style, and angry rap backed by drum machines and screaming guitars, marked the end of the old-school style. In 1985, they were the only rap group to perform at the charity concert Live Aid. The fatal shooting of Jay in 2002 sadly spelled the end for Run-DMC.

CONCERT

At a concert in Madison Square Garden, New York, Run-DMC asked the 20,000 audience members to raise their Adidas trainers for 'My Adidas'.

GREATEST HIT

'Walk This Way', a duo performed with rock band Aerosmith, was the fusion hit of 1986.

SELECTED DISCOGRAPHY

1985
King of Rock

1986
Raising Hell

1988
Tougher than Leather

1990
Back from Hell

2012
The Essential Run-DMC

ROCK & HIP-HOP

Following their first album, Run-DMC pushed fierce guitar riffs by Eddie Martinez up against rap beats. In the video for 'King of Rock', Run and DMC impersonate and mock the Beatles.

MAINSTREAM

With 15 million albums sold, Run-DMC were among the first to make hip-hop successful on a big scale. They were also the first hip-hop group to appear on the cover of the magazine *Rolling Stone*.

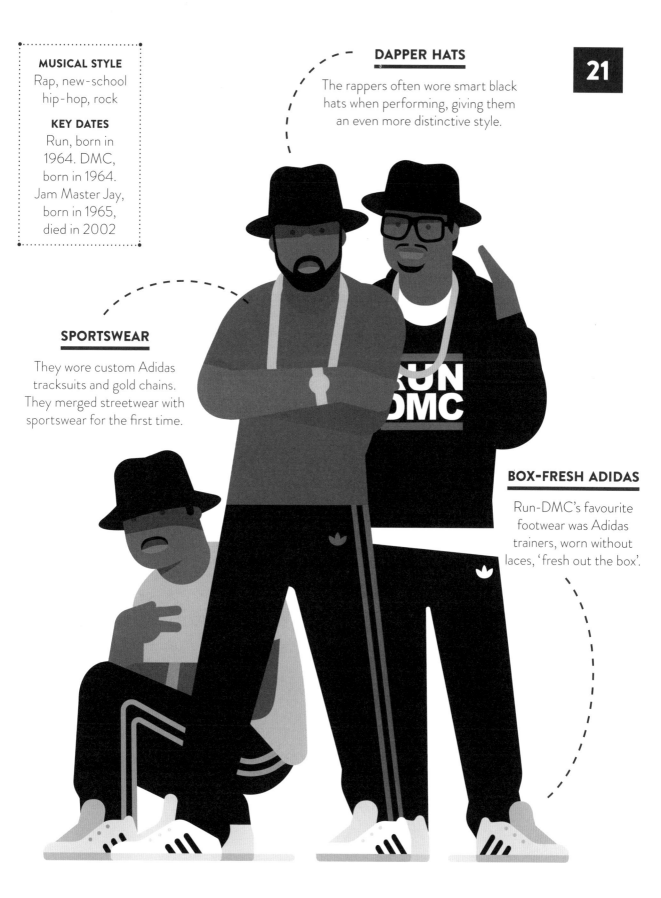

MUSICAL STYLE
Rap, new-school hip-hop, rock

KEY DATES
Run, born in 1964. DMC, born in 1964. Jam Master Jay, born in 1965, died in 2002

DAPPER HATS
The rappers often wore smart black hats when performing, giving them an even more distinctive style.

SPORTSWEAR
They wore custom Adidas tracksuits and gold chains. They merged streetwear with sportswear for the first time.

BOX-FRESH ADIDAS
Run-DMC's favourite footwear was Adidas trainers, worn without laces, 'fresh out the box'.

Hardcore rappers of the 1980s

Eric B. & Rakim

CULT ALBUM

In 2006, *Paid In Full* was named the 'greatest hip-hop album of all time' by MTV music channel.

Eric B. is a DJ and Rakim is a rapper and they are both from New York. The duo released their first single, 'Eric B is President', in 1986 and it was an instant hit. Critics said Rakim's revolutionary vocal style influenced hip-hop to come and their first album *Paid in Full* is a rap classic. Rakim's powerful storytelling paints a picture of his youth growing up on the block, signalling the arrival of the gangsta rap genre. The duo separated in 1992, but Rakim continued to make music on his own.

RISKY REMIX

The song 'Paid in Full' is a song from Eric B. & Rakim's album of the same name. In 1987 it was remixed by the English group Coldcut. It was a hit in France but Eric B. hated it and said it made him look like a clown.

SELECTED DISCOGRAPHY

1987
Paid in Full

1988
Follow the Leader

1990
Let the Rhythm Hit'em

1992
Don't Sweat the Technique

2008
Repaid in Full: The Paid in Full Remixed

SCANDAL

Due to legal problems following the break-up of the group, Rakim had to wait five years before he could release his solo album, *The 18th Letter*.

REUNION

After 23 years apart, the duo announced they were re-grouping in October 2016. Despite not yet releasing a new album, in July 2017 they performed at the Apollo Theater in New York.

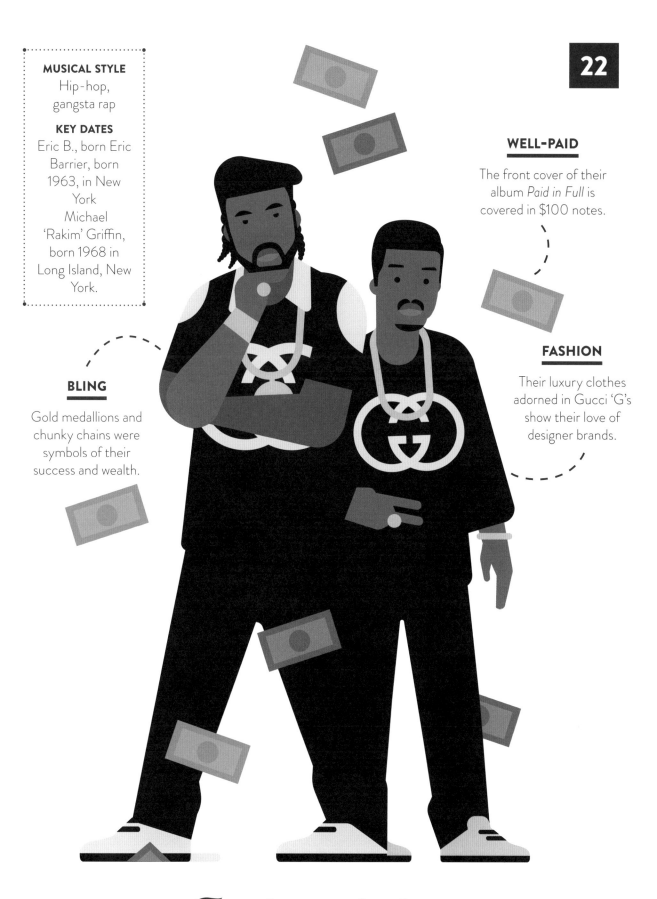

MUSICAL STYLE
Hip-hop,
gangsta rap

KEY DATES
Eric B., born Eric
Barrier, born
1963, in New
York
Michael
'Rakim' Griffin,
born 1968 in
Long Island, New
York.

22

WELL-PAID

The front cover of their
album *Paid in Full* is
covered in $100 notes.

FASHION

Their luxury clothes
adorned in Gucci 'G's
show their love of
designer brands.

BLING

Gold medallions and
chunky chains were
symbols of their
success and wealth.

The dynamic duo

Public Enemy

Since their first album launched in 1987, Public Enemy have made waves with their bold, dense sound and outspoken lyrics, produced with hip-hop production team the Bomb Squad. Chuck D is the lead singer of the group, Flavor Flav the joker, and their shows always cause a stir, with one featuring dancers dressed in military uniform carrying uzis (submachine guns). Their ferocious musical force has influenced artists like Nirvana. More than 30 years after their debut, Public Enemy still tour the world.

SCANDAL
In the rap 'Burn Hollywood Burn', Public Enemy criticised the cinema industry, who only give black actors supporting and baddie roles.

FIVE DATES

1983
Chuck D meets Flavor Flav.

1987
Def Jam label release their first album *Yo! Bum Rush the Show.*

1989
'Fight the Power' commissioned for Spike Lee's film *Do the Right Thing.*

1998
Terminator X leaves to start an ostrich farm.

2015
Release *Man Plans God Laughs* album.

GREATEST HIT

'Fight the Power' became a huge hit, referencing civil rights issues, gospel church services and the music of James Brown. It is often listed as one of the best songs of the century.

HEAVY RAP
Public Enemy joined forces with heavy metal group Anthrax in 1991 to re-record their hit record 'Bring the Noise'. The two groups then toured together in 1992.

MILITANT
In 1991, as a protest against the US government's refusal to create a federal holiday for Martin Luther King, Public Enemy released 'By the Time I Get to Arizona'. The video for the song imagines the assassination of Arizona's governor.

23

MUSICAL STYLE
Rap, hip-hop fusion, rock

KEY DATES
Chuck D born Carlton Ridenhour in 1960.
Flavor Flav born William Drayton in 1959.
Terminator X born Norman Rogers in 1966.

THE RIGHT TIME
Flavor Flav wears a giant clock slung around his neck, because he knows 'what time it is'.

BLACK POWER
With fists raised in the Black Power salute, Public Enemy raised consciousness.

LOGO
The group's logo is a black man at the centre of the crosshairs of a gun. It symbolises the dangers of being black in America.

Fight the power

N.W.A

N.W.A came straight out of Compton, the most notorious district in Los Angeles. N.W.A (Niggaz Wit Attitudes) created Californian gangsta rap: melodic rap paired with explicit lyrics. They released a song criticising the police, which got them in trouble with the FBI, while it also earned them worldwide fame. N.W.A split up after the release of their second album in 1991, *Efil4zaggin* (*Niggaz 4 Life* written in reverse). Dr. Dre became Snoop Dogg and Eminem's producer, Ice Cube an actor and producer, while Eazy-E, the group's founder, died of AIDs in 1995.

THREE DATES

1988
Debut album, *Straight Outta Compton*, launches.

1993
Dr. Dre produces Snoop Dogg's *Doggystyle*.

2006
Jerry Heller, the ex-manager of N.W.A, releases his biography, *Ruthless: A Memoir*.

SCANDAL

They released a song protesting against the police which was banned from being played on the radio, and N.W.A were prevented from performing it live.

ON THE BIG SCREEN

In 2015, a film telling the story of N.W.A brought in $200 million in sales. Entitled *Straight Outta Compton*, it traced the group's journey to fame and its notorious disputes with management.

SYMBOLIC

The cover of N.W.A's single *Gangsta Gangsta* depicts a young white man stealing the rapper Ice Cube's trainers – turning the tables on the stereotype of young black men as trainer thieves.

CULT ALBUM

Straight Outta Compton is the legendary album by 'the world's most dangerous group'.

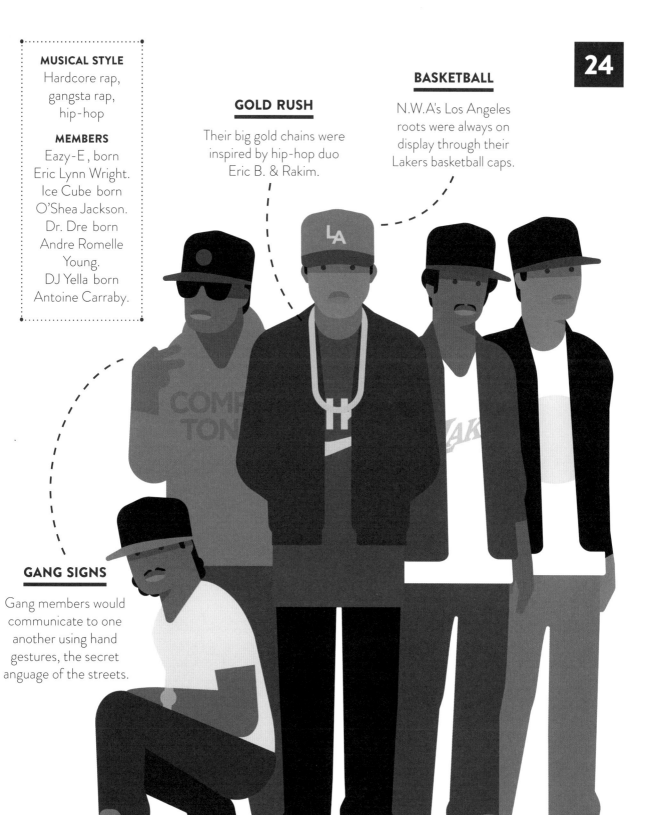

24

MUSICAL STYLE
Hardcore rap,
gangsta rap,
hip-hop

MEMBERS
Eazy-E , born
Eric Lynn Wright.
Ice Cube born
O'Shea Jackson.
Dr. Dre born
Andre Romelle
Young.
DJ Yella born
Antoine Carraby.

GOLD RUSH
Their big gold chains were
inspired by hip-hop duo
Eric B. & Rakim.

BASKETBALL
N.W.A's Los Angeles
roots were always on
display through their
Lakers basketball caps.

GANG SIGNS
Gang members would
communicate to one
another using hand
gestures, the secret
anguage of the streets.

The inventors of gangsta rap

Whitney Houston

At 11 years old, Whitney Houston was singing gospel solos in her local church. Aged 22, she released her first album, which was the biggest seller by a female artist of the 1980s. Gifted with an exceptional voice, Houston launched a cinema career, starring in *The Bodyguard* alongside Kevin Costner and also singing the soundtrack, which featured her greatest hit, 'I Will Always Love You'. Following her marriage to the singer Bobby Brown, Houston's lifestyle became chaotic and troubled. She died suddenly at 48.

DRAMA

In 2010, during Houston's *Nothing But Love World Tour*, disaster struck as the singer lost her voice, causing almost all the shows to be cancelled.

BESTSELLER

Written by Dolly Parton, 'I Will Always Love You' stayed at the top of the American charts for 14 weeks in the autumn of 1992.

SELECTED DISCOGRAPHY

1985
Whitney Houston

1990
I'm Your Baby Tonight

1998
My Love Is Your Love

2002
Just Whitney...

2009
I Look to You

HOMAGE

On 18 February 2012, at Houston's funeral, many black music greats performed eulogies for her, including Stevie Wonder, Alicia Keys (who worked with Houston on her last album) and R. Kelly.

MOVIE STAR

In 1992, in order to play the lead in the film *The Bodyguard*, Houston had to audition multiple times to prove to the producers that she could act as well as she could sing. She was finally given the role by Kevin Costner, the film's hero.

25

SUPER-SMILE

Houston's dazzling smile always seemed to light up the room.

DIVA DUET

Houston sang with fellow diva Mariah Carey in 1998 for the soundtrack to the animated film *The Prince of Egypt*.

STRATOSPHERIC SUCCESS

'The success of "I Will Always Love You" took my career to a whole new level'.

MUSICAL STYLE
Soul, pop, gospel, disco, R&B

KEY DATES
Born in 1963, died in 2012

The voice of R&B

2 Pac

Born in Brooklyn, Tupac Shakur, also known as 2Pac, embodied gangsta rap and became a hip-hop legend. Raised by his mother, who was a Black Panther, 2Pac started his music career by joining the group Digital Underground. He went on to launch his solo career and signed to Death Row Records with Dr. Dre. There he released *All Eyez on Me*, a double CD, just a few months before being fatally shot in Las Vegas at the age of 25, in 1996. A prolific writer in the studio, 20 2Pac albums were released after his death.

A NEW NAME

Just before his death, 2Pac decided to changed his name to Makaveli, having just read Niccolò Machiavelli's famous work *The Prince*.

SELECTED DISCOGRAPHY

1991
2Pacalypse Now

1995
Me Against the World

1996
All Eyez on Me

2004
Loyal to the Game

2006
Pac's Life

BACKGROUND
Born in New York, 2Pac lived in Los Angeles and was killed in Las Vegas.

LOVE HATE RELATIONSHIP

Having moved to California, 2Pac became a sworn enemy of his former best friend Notorious B.I.G., the New York rapper. 2Pac goaded and dissed Biggie in many of his tracks.

ACTIVISM
2Pac sung about the treatment of black people and defended feminism, as in the song 'Brenda's Got a Baby', which is about young single mothers.

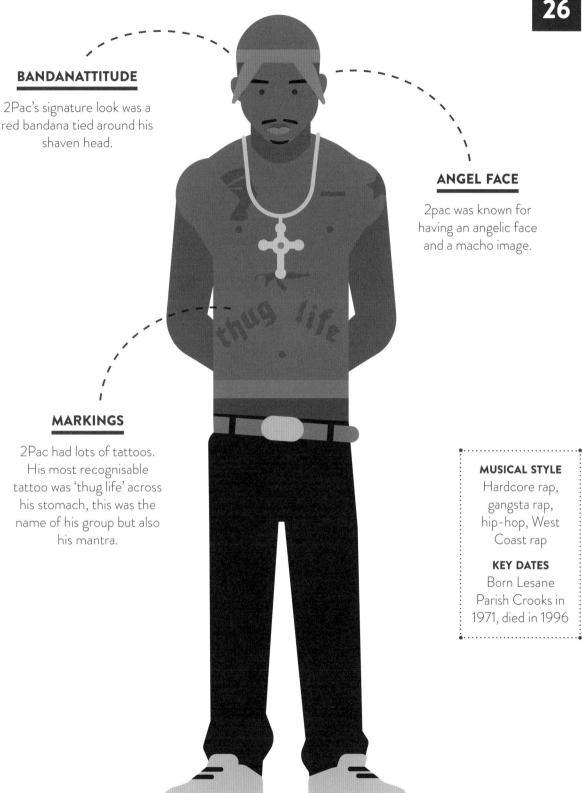

26

BANDANATTITUDE

2Pac's signature look was a red bandana tied around his shaven head.

ANGEL FACE

2pac was known for having an angelic face and a macho image.

MARKINGS

2Pac had lots of tattoos. His most recognisable tattoo was 'thug life' across his stomach, this was the name of his group but also his mantra.

MUSICAL STYLE
Hardcore rap, gangsta rap, hip-hop, West Coast rap

KEY DATES
Born Lesane Parish Crooks in 1971, died in 1996

The fallen angel

The Fugees

GREATEST HIT

'Killing Me Softly', Lauryn Hill's cover of a Roberta Flack song, became a universal hit in 1996.

BORROWING

For their single 'Ready or Not' the Fugees used a sample from the singer Enya without her permission.

Wyclef Jean and Pras are originally from Haiti, and Lauryn Hill is from California. The Fugees released their first album, *Blunted on Reality*, in 1994. Two years later, they exploded onto the scene with *The Score*, a melodic mix of rap, soul and reggae. Featuring a cover of Bob Marley's 'No Woman No Cry', the record sold 20 million copies and was the Fugees' last group project. Hill wowed the world with her debut *The Miseducation of Lauryn Hill*, while Wyclef founded an NGO called Yéle Haiti Foundation funding disaster relief in Haiti.

FIVE DATES

1990
Wyclef Jean meets Lauryn Hill and Pras.

1996
The Score is released.

1997
Win two awards at the Grammys.

1998
Lauryn Hill releases her first solo album.

2005
Group tour for the last time.

INFLUENCES

The Fugees were inspired by the music of Bob Marley, as well as by soul and rap music.

ON THE BIG SCREEN

In 2004, the Fugees reunited in Brooklyn to participate in a concert organised by the comedian Dave Chappelle and filmed by French director Michel Gondry for the documentary *Dave Chappelle's Block Party*.

27

MUSICAL STYLE
Rap, soul, reggae, world music, hip-hop

KEY DATES
Lauryn Hill born in 1975. Wyclef Jean born in 1969. Pras Michel born in 1972

THREE MUSKETEERS

A voice like honey, a cool customer and a worldly activist: Lauryn, Pras and Wyclef make up the Fugees.

'NO WOMAN NO CRY'

Wyclef, the Haitian New Yorker, identified with Bob Marley and covered one of his classics.

INSTRUMENTAL RAP

'When we recorded *The Score* it was unlike anything else being made at the time.'
—Wyclef Jean

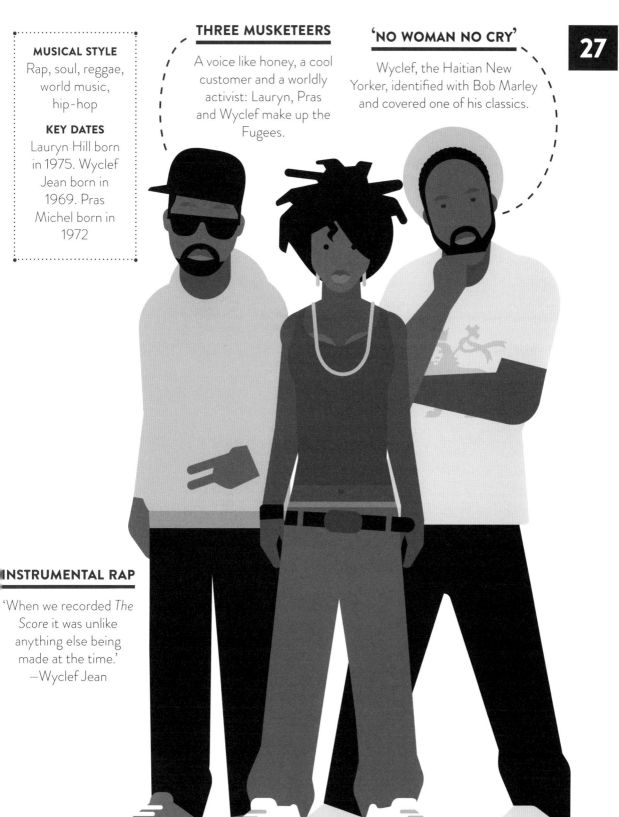

The rap-reggae trio

Snoop Dogg

The most famous representative of California rap, Snoop kicked off his career with *Doggystyle*, his multi-platinum debut album produced by Dr. Dre. His laidback, smooth musical style has made him a hero of the West Coast, which stands in contrast to the more authentic and less commercial sounds of New York (East Coast). A long way from the violent neighbourhoods where he grew up, now also an actor and sports coach with his own cookery show, Snoop remains a West Coast hip-hop icon.

SCANDAL

Following the release of his first album, Snoop was charged with murder. He was eventually found not guilty.

GREATEST HIT

Produced and performed with Pharrell Williams, 'Beautiful' won three Grammy awards at the 2003 ceremony.

ON THE BIG SCREEN

Snoop has appeared in more than 30 films, including *The Wash* with Eminem and *Pitch Perfect 2*. His voice is also used in the animated film *Arthur and the Invisibles*.

AVATAR

In 2012, Snoop Dogg briefly transformed into 'Snoop Lion' for the release of his new album *Reincarnated*, which was influenced by reggae and produced by Major Lazer.

SELECTED DISCOGRAPHY

1993
Doggystyle

1996
Tha Doggfather

2002
Paid tha Cost to Be da Boss

2006
Tha Blue Carpet Treatment

2017
Neva Left

28

COACH SNOOP

Snoop Dogg is a huge sports fan and is head coach of his son's football team.

PLAITED HAIR

Snoop's braids, styled in different variations, are unmistakeable.

MUSICAL STYLE
G-funk, rap, gangsta rap, hip-hop

KEY DATES
Born Calvin Broadus in 1971

ROYAL BLUE

Snoop often wears blue, the colour of his gang, the Crips.

West Coast Dogg

The Notorious B.I.G.

Sometimes referred to as **Biggie Smalls, the Notorious B.I.G. – born** Christopher Wallace – was catapulted into fame with his first album, *Ready to Die*. Biggie has a huge stature, a powerful voice and unparalleled talent. With his producer, P. Diddy, Biggie became a respected artist. However, his disagreements with 2Pac escalated into all-out war as East Coast clashed with West Coast. Initially, the battles took the form of songs, but they soon turned to real violence. Rivals 2Pac and Biggie were both murdered within six months of each other.

INFLUENCES

Biggie was a lover of old-school American rap, in particular Big Daddy Kane and Heavy D.

GREATEST HIT

'Juicy', featuring a sample from 'Juicy Fruit' by Mtume, is where rap meets pop. Produced by P. Diddy, it is Biggie at his best.

SELECTED DISCOGRAPHY

1994
Ready to Die

1997
Life After Death

1999
Born Again

2005
Duets: the Final Chapter

2009
Notorious

IMPROVISATION

Grand MC (meaning 'master of ceremony'), Biggie loved to rap live, without writing his lyrics down on paper. He would sit for two hours, then suddenly stand-up, move to the microphone and perform his rap.

FAMILY

Biggie married the R&B singer Faith Evans, with whom he had a son, Christopher Jr, who was born just four months before his father was killed in a drive-by shooting.

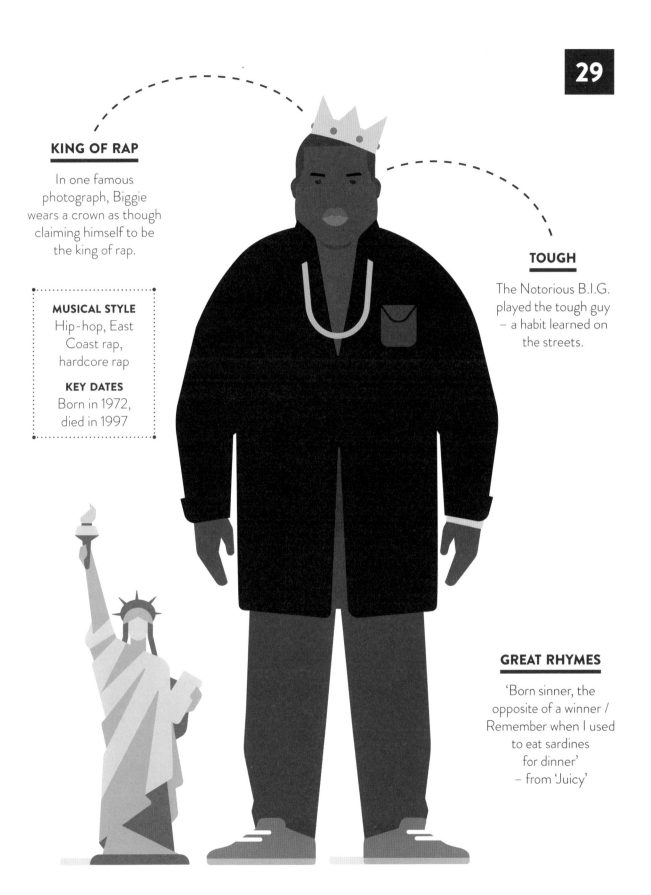

29

KING OF RAP

In one famous photograph, Biggie wears a crown as though claiming himself to be the king of rap.

MUSICAL STYLE
Hip-hop, East Coast rap, hardcore rap

KEY DATES
Born in 1972, died in 1997

TOUGH

The Notorious B.I.G. played the tough guy – a habit learned on the streets.

GREAT RHYMES

'Born sinner, the opposite of a winner / Remember when I used to eat sardines for dinner' – from 'Juicy'

Sublime king of rhyme

Erykah Badu

A native of Texas, Erykah Badu started her career in 1994. When she was 23 a producer spotted her talent and three years later she had released her album *Baduizm,* which was a sensation. People loved her eccentric style and enchanting voice and she became known as one of the key figures in a genre called neo-soul. This was a form of contemporary R&B tinted with shades of hip-hop. Badu was very politically engaged and for this reason she is often compared to Billie Holiday.

THREE DATES

1985
Freestyles for the first time on a Dallas radio station.

6 February 1998
Acts in the film *Blues Brothers 2000,* playing Queen Moussette.

20 August 2002
Releases *Love Of My Life (An Ode To Hip-Hop),* winner of the best music video of the year at the BET Awards.

COME BACK

In 2015, Erykah made a return, putting out her own remixed version of Drake's 'Hotline Bling', which she included on her mixtape *But You Caint Use My Phone.* The original Drake song is 4 minutes 30 seconds long, but Badu's bumper edition lasts 7 minutes 25 seconds!

LEGENDARY CONCERT

In 2004, Erykah sang at the concert organised by comedian Dave Chappelle in his Brooklyn neighbourhood of New York. The show was filmed by Michel Gondry and released in cinemas as *Dave Chappelle's Block Party.*

30

ACTIVISM

Her afro hair tied up
with a scarf is a homage
to the black political
heroines of the 1970s.

DETERMINATION

Her fierce look – that of
a free woman in control
– signals Badu's refusal
to be objectified.

AFRICAN

Badu's African jewellery shows
the Egyptian symbol of the
ankh in gold.

MUSICAL STYLE
Neo-soul, R&B,
hip-hop

KEY DATES
Born 26 February
1971 in Dallas,
Texas.

Queen of Neo-Soul

Jay-Z

BACKGROUND

Jay-Z comes from Brooklyn, New York, or more precisely, from Marcy Projects, a public-housing project known for violence and crime.

Jay-Z was born Shawn Carter in Brooklyn. He has become known as one of the best rappers of his generation. After his first album, *Reasonable Doubt*, he released a string of albums including two duets, with R. Kelly and then with Kanye West. In his career he has sold over 100 million albums and won 21 Grammy awards. His success took him to the White House as a guest of US president Barack Obama. He is married to the superstar Beyoncé and together they form one of the most prolific power couples of music.

BEYONCÉ

Jay-Z married Beyoncé in April 2008 and the couple toured together in 2014. Their *On the Run Tour* made them $110 million.

SELECTED DISCOGRAPHY

1997
In My Lifetime Vol. 1

1998
Vol. 2 Hard Knock Life

2001
The Blueprint

2003
The Black Album

2011
Watch the Throne (with Kanye West)

ACTIVISM

Jay-Z campaigned for the election of Barack Obama in the American presidential races of 2008 and 2012, and for Hillary Clinton in 2016.

BUSINESS

Jay-Z launched the label Roc-A-Fella Records, was director of Def Jam Records, launched a sportswear line, Rocawear, while owning half of the Brooklyn Nets basketball team. As he would say, 'I am not a businessman, I'm a business, man!'

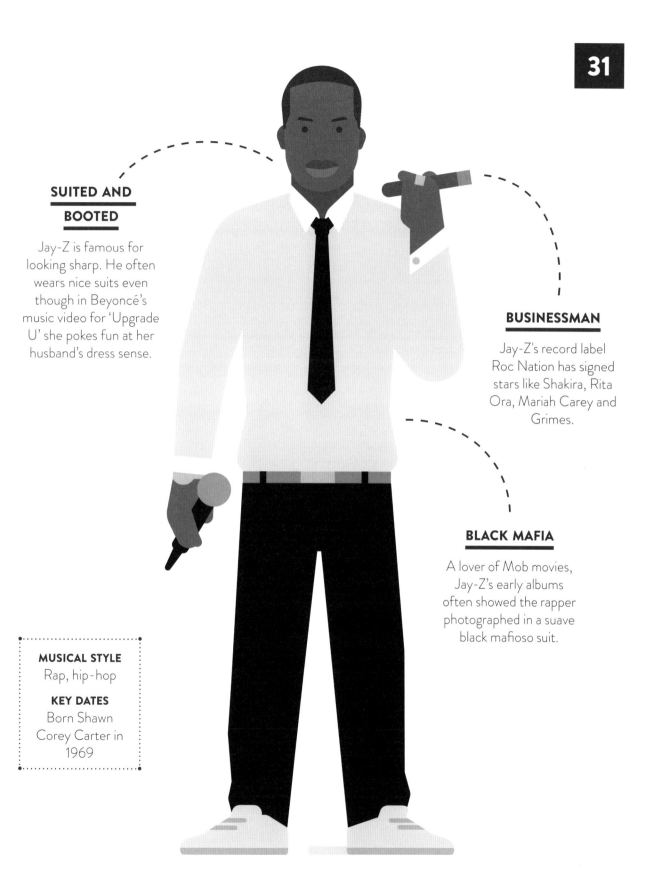

31

SUITED AND BOOTED

Jay-Z is famous for looking sharp. He often wears nice suits even though in Beyoncé's music video for 'Upgrade U' she pokes fun at her husband's dress sense.

BUSINESSMAN

Jay-Z's record label Roc Nation has signed stars like Shakira, Rita Ora, Mariah Carey and Grimes.

BLACK MAFIA

A lover of Mob movies, Jay-Z's early albums often showed the rapper photographed in a suave black mafioso suit.

MUSICAL STYLE
Rap, hip-hop

KEY DATES
Born Shawn Corey Carter in 1969

The boss of New York

Missy Elliott

Missy 'Misdemeanor' Elliott grew up singing with her mother in church. At 20, she formed an all-female group called Sista, before launching her solo career with the help of producer Timbaland, her childhood friend, with whom she would record her first album *Supa Dupa Fly*. Her big hit, 'The Rain', showed the world how Elliott was an extraordinary rapper. A strong woman, her lyrics argued for female independence. In 2011, she explained a long absence from the music industry as being caused by her long term illness hyperthyroidism.

REVERSE IT

The hit song 'Work It' features a line played in reverse that sounds like gibberish, but if you played it forwards it makes sense.

ACTIVISM

In her 2015 song 'Where They From' Missy makes it clear that she thinks women deserve more respect.

THE BEST

Missy Elliott released three hit albums in three years. This secured her position as the best-selling female rapper of all time – a title she has hung onto since the early 2000s.

SELECTED DISCOGRAPHY

1997
Supa Dupa Fly

1999
Da Real World

2001
Miss E... So Addictive

2002
Under Construction

2005
The Cookbook

PAVING THE WAY

Many female pop stars credit Missy Elliott as paving the way for their own expressions of feminism. These include Beyoncé and Nicki Minaj.

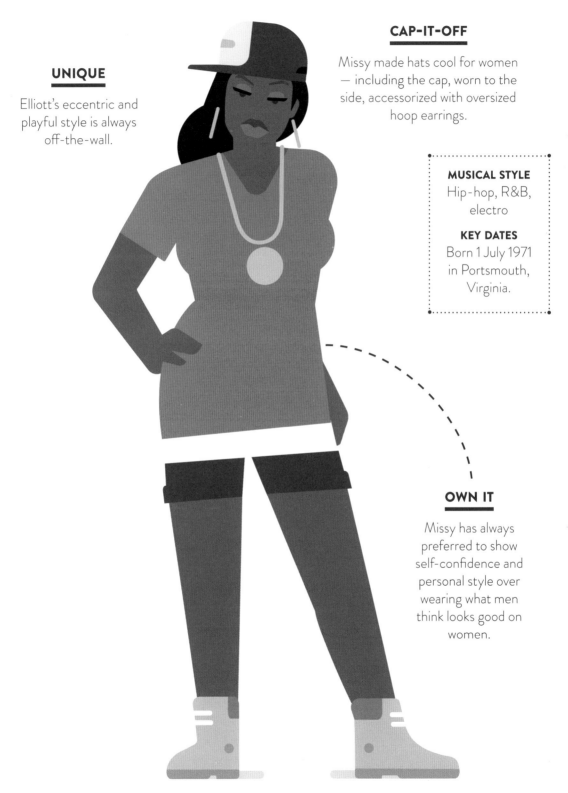

32

CAP-IT-OFF

Missy made hats cool for women — including the cap, worn to the side, accessorized with oversized hoop earrings.

UNIQUE

Elliott's eccentric and playful style is always off-the-wall.

MUSICAL STYLE
Hip-hop, R&B, electro

KEY DATES
Born 1 July 1971 in Portsmouth, Virginia.

OWN IT

Missy has always preferred to show self-confidence and personal style over wearing what men think looks good on women.

A rapper and a feminist

Kanye West

CONCERT

On 17 November 2007, Kanye played the Zénith in Paris, one week after his mother's death. He broke down in tears during the song 'Hey Mamma'.

Born in Atlanta, but raised in Chicago, Kanye West first made a name for himself with his 2004 album *The College Dropout*. As talented as he is intolerably egocentric, Kanye popularised Autotune software, which he used in 2008 on his album *808s & Heartbreak*. The *New York Times* wrote of West, both a lover and designer of luxury fashion 'No rapper has embodied hip-hop's often contradictory impulses of narcissism and social good quite as he has...'

FROM RAP TO ROCK

Open to all genres, Kanye has twice collaborated with former Beatle Paul McCartney, as well as with French electro duo Daft Punk, who he sampled on his track 'Stronger' and who he later asked to co-produce his album *Yeezus*.

SELECTED DISCOGRAPHY

2005
Late Registration

2007
Graduation

2010
My Beautiful Dark Twisted Fantasy

2013
Yeezus

2016
The Life Of Pablo

KANYE FOR PRESIDENT

In 2015, during a surreal speech at the Video Music Awards, West declared that he would run for president in the 2020 elections. He also met Donald Trump just before he was made president in December 2016.

INFLUENCES

West has proclaimed his admiration for Marvin Gaye, Gil Scott-Heron, David Bowie, P. Diddy, Madonna, Michael Jackson and Phil Collins.

33

MUSICAL STYLE
Hip-hop, soul, pop, rap, R&B

KEY DATES
Born Kanye Omari West in 1977

FASHION
Married to the celebrity Kim Kardashian, Kanye is often seen sitting in the front row at fashion week.

FUR COAT
West's eccentricity and originality is made plain in his choice of lavish and creative clothing.

BOOTS (FOR WALKING)
His trusty Timberland boots are a sign that, despite his fame, he always keeps his feet firmly on the ground.

The dapper rapper

Beyoncé

Beyoncé Knowles joined the girl group Destiny's Child at the age of 15. In 2002, she won a role in the box-office hit *Austin Powers: Goldmember* and later that year released her debut album *Dangerously in Love*, which won 5 Grammy awards. A proud feminist, Queen Bey sings about women and independence in 'Single Ladies' and 'If I Were a Boy'. She is often presented as Rihanna's ultimate rival, although her career has been much longer and more varied. Beyoncé has sold over 160 million records in under 20 years.

ACTIVISM

In her cinematic music video for 'Lemonade', Bey uses imagery inspired by the Black Panthers and pledges her allegiance to the Black Lives Matter movement.

FIVE DATES

1987
Attends a transformative Michael Jackson concert.

1993
Appears on *Star Search*.

2003
Releases first song with Jay-Z, *03 Bonnie & Clyde*.

2008
Marries Jay-Z.

2018
Performs at Coachella, one year late due to pregnancy.

CONCERT

In 2011, Beyoncé was the first ever female headliner at Glastonbury music festival.

BLACK LIVES MATTER

A vocal supporter of Black Lives Matter, a movement led by families of young black men and women wrongfully killed by American police officers. She shows her support in her video for her single 'Freedom'.

BLING BEY

With an estimated wealth of $1.16 billion, the Beyoncé/Jay-Z marital enterprise tops the list, making them the world's richest pop stars. Between 2009 and 2011, Beyoncé earned $70 million per year!

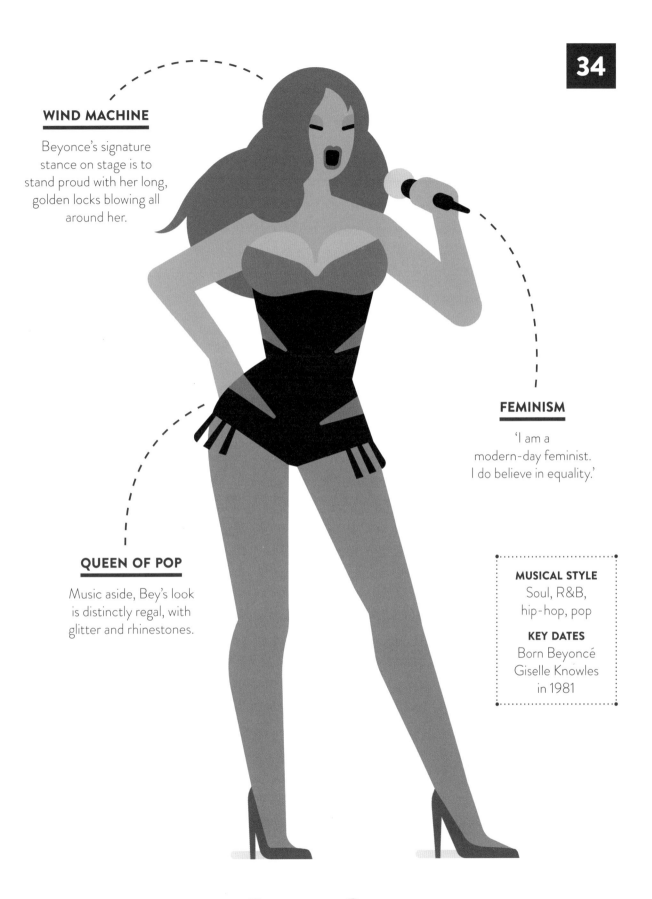

34

WIND MACHINE

Beyonce's signature
stance on stage is to
stand proud with her long,
golden locks blowing all
around her.

FEMINISM

'I am a
modern-day feminist.
I do believe in equality.'

QUEEN OF POP

Music aside, Bey's look
is distinctly regal, with
glitter and rhinestones.

MUSICAL STYLE
Soul, R&B,
hip-hop, pop

KEY DATES
Born Beyoncé
Giselle Knowles
in 1981

Queen Bey

Pharrell Williams

FIVE DATES

1992
Forms The Neptunes with Chad Hugo.

2001
Produces *I'm a Slave 4 U* for Britney Spears.

2004
Features on Snoop Dogg's *Drop It Like It's Hot*.

2006
Releases first solo album, *In My Mind*.

2014
Joins the judging panel for the US version of The Voice.

With his school friend Chad Hugo, Pharrell Williams founded The Neptunes, a band and music production duo who have worked with Britney Spears, Snoop Dogg, Kelis, Justin Timberlake and many of the world's most famous artists. As a solo artist, Pharrell is known for making pop music to dance to, with funky rhythms and sunny vocals. His love of fashion has seen him create his own label, Billionaire Boys Club, and work with brands like Louis Vuitton and artist Takashi Murakami. In 2013, he featured on Daft Punk's 'Get Lucky'.

GREATEST HIT

Pharrell went multi-platinum with his single 'Happy', written as the soundtrack to the computer-animated film, *Despicable Me 2*.

'BLURRED LINES'

Williams performs with the rapper T.I. on the bestseller song 'Blurred Lines' by Robin Thicke. Williams and Thicke were taken to court by the family of Marvin Gaye, who accused them of copying Gaye's music without permission.

VIRAL

In 2013, as part of the promotion for Pharrell's single 'Happy', the world's first 24-hour music video went live online. It featured celebrities and ordinary people dancing to the song 360 times over throughout the streets of LA.

INFLUENCES

A Tribe Called Quest's first album from 1990 was what made Williams understand how 'music was art'.

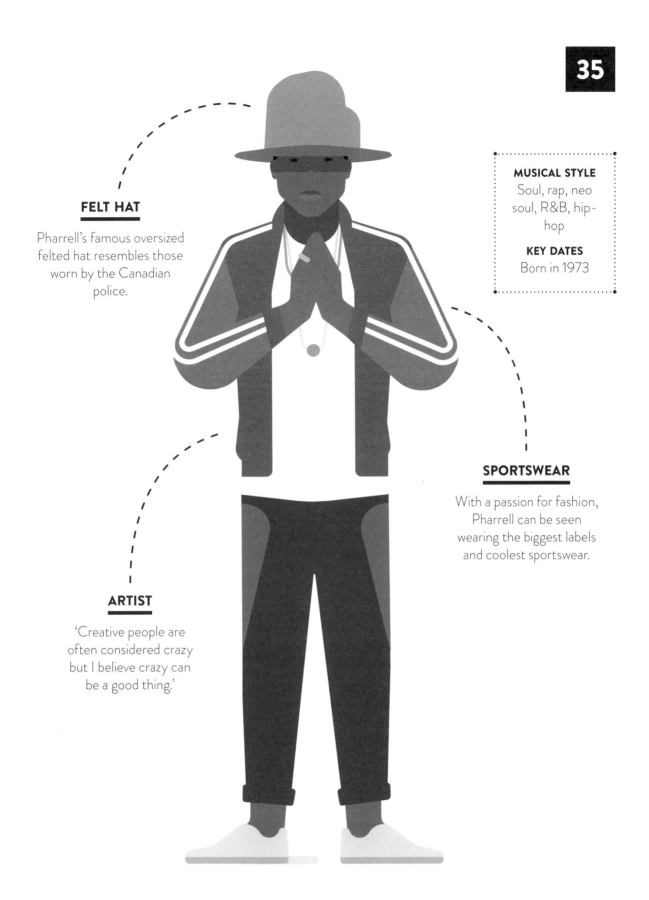

35

FELT HAT

Pharrell's famous oversized felted hat resembles those worn by the Canadian police.

MUSICAL STYLE
Soul, rap, neo soul, R&B, hip-hop

KEY DATES
Born in 1973

SPORTSWEAR

With a passion for fashion, Pharrell can be seen wearing the biggest labels and coolest sportswear.

ARTIST

'Creative people are often considered crazy but I believe crazy can be a good thing.'

The fashion addict

Rihanna

Rihanna was born on the island of Barbados in the Caribnean, but left aged 15 for the United States.

Originating from the Caribbean, **Rihanna was signed to Def Jam** Records by none other than Jay-Z himself. Her list of achievements is lengthy: 54 million albums sold across the world, 8 Grammy awards, 14 number-one singles and second place in a poll of the most popular singers (she came second to Madonna). With her iconic style, Rihanna is both a trendsetter and star of social media (she has more than 50 million Instagram followers).

IN LOVE

She once dated the singer Chris Brown, but the 'dream couple' broke up after Brown violently attacked Rihanna, forcing her to cancel her Grammy's performance. Since then she is rumoured to have dated Drake and Travis Scott.

SELECTED DISCOGRAPHY

2005
Music of the Sun

2007
Good Girl Gone Bad

2009
Rated R

2010
Loud

2016
Anti

GREATEST HIT

In 2007, Rihanna gained fans across the world with her single 'Umbrella'. At the top of the charts in 13 countries, it features Jay-Z.

BUSINESS

In 2015, Rihanna announced she had become a shareholder of Tidal, the high-end streaming service taken over by Jay-Z. Its other investors include Daft Punk, Madonna, Nicki Minaj, Kanye West, and Beyoncé among others.

36

MUSICAL STYLE
R&B, electro, pop, dance music, reggae

KEY DATES
Born Robyn Rihanna Fenty in 1988

HAIR-RAISING

Rihanna's hairstyle changes with every new album release: from braids to afro, fringe to curly mane.

TATTOOS

Rihanna's many tattoos grace the cover of her album *Unapologetic* (2012).

CONFIDENCE

'I actually like my body... I just feel sexy.'

The pop-star provocateur

Lil Wayne

Signed to the record label Cash Money Records at the age of just 9, Lil Wayne is a rap prodigy who has released 15 albums, 20 mixtapes and more than 200 singles! First a member of Hot Boys before becoming a solo artist, Lil Wayne has an original vocal style. Hungry for the microphone, he has received critical acclaim for all his albums, notably for his *Tha Carter* series. Barack Obama even referred to him in a 2009 speech: 'They might think they've got a pretty jump shot or a pretty good flow but our kids can't all aspire to be LeBron or Lil Wayne.'

ROCK

In 2010, Lil Wayne, whose favourite group is Nirvana, tried his hand at rock for his seventh album, *Rebirth*, full of heavy guitar riffs. His video for 'Prom Queen' featured the band Korn.

DIRTY SOUTH

Lil Wayne's style of hip-hop – known as Dirty South – originates in the Southern states of the US. Its sound is jarring, jerky and modern. Other Southern stars include OutKast, Migos and Lil Jon.

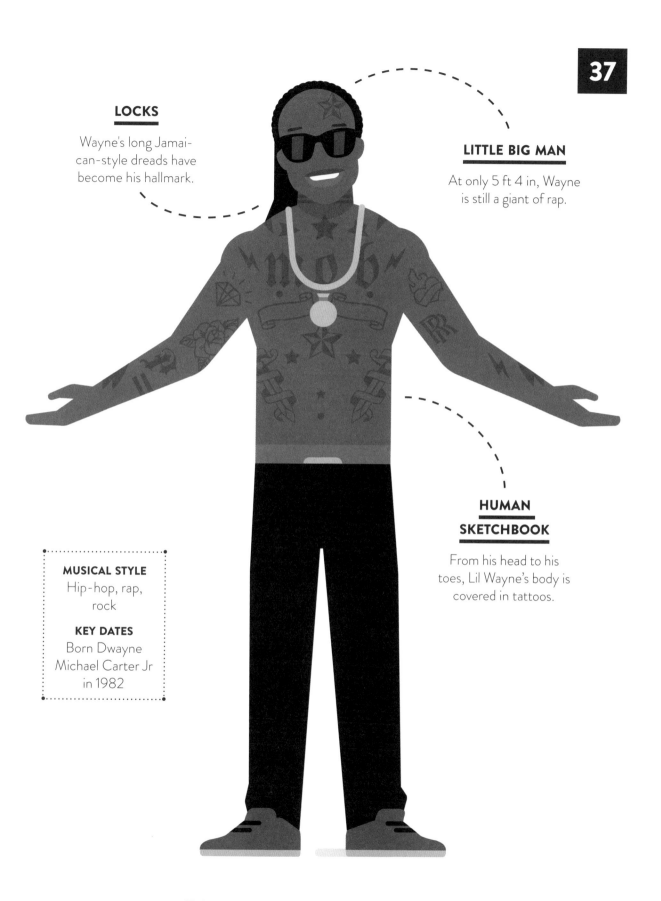

37

LOCKS

Wayne's long Jamaican-style dreads have become his hallmark.

LITTLE BIG MAN

At only 5 ft 4 in, Wayne is still a giant of rap.

MUSICAL STYLE
Hip-hop, rap, rock

KEY DATES
Born Dwayne Michael Carter Jr in 1982

HUMAN SKETCHBOOK

From his head to his toes, Lil Wayne's body is covered in tattoos.

The inked innovator

Drake

Drake made his name through mixtapes. His blending of rap with soft vocals creates a melodic, melancholic dynamism – the secret to his successful album *Nothing Was the Same* (2013), which featured collaborations with Jay-Z and Sampha. Although shy of the world's media, his social media tells a different story (he has 37 million Instagram followers), while his video for 'Hotline Bling' was a viral sensation and provoked thousands of parodies across the internet. In 2017, his album *Views* won two Grammys.

CULT ALBUM

Nothing Was the Same is Drake's signature album, with 'Started from the Bottom' his trademark track.

BACKGROUND

Drake grew up in Toronto, which he refers to as 'The 6' in many songs.

TORONTO

In 2013, Drake became the official ambassador for the NBA Toronto Raptors basketball team. The Mayor of Toronto has also honoured the star by presenting him with the key to the city.

LAUGH & CRY

Behind his sweet smile, Drake is a fierce battle rapper, and has had arguments with Kid Cudi, Jay-Z, Kendrick Lamar, Common, Ludacris and Pusha T. A comedy fan too, his basketball sketch with the actor Will Ferrell is legendary.

SELECTED DISCOGRAPHY

2000
Thank Me Later

2011
Take Care

2015
If You're Reading This It's Too Late

2016
Views

2017
More Life

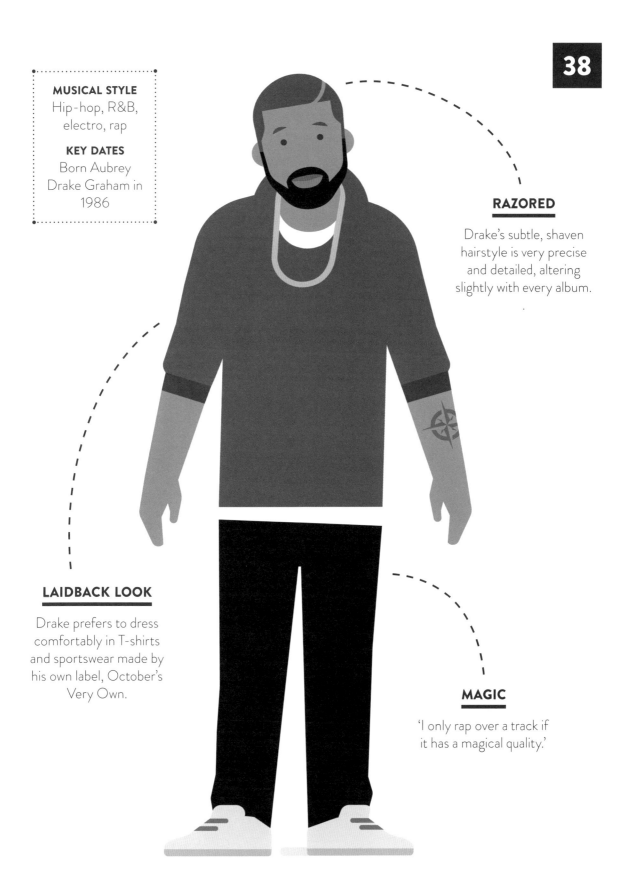

38

MUSICAL STYLE
Hip-hop, R&B, electro, rap

KEY DATES
Born Aubrey Drake Graham in 1986

RAZORED

Drake's subtle, shaven hairstyle is very precise and detailed, altering slightly with every album.
.

LAIDBACK LOOK

Drake prefers to dress comfortably in T-shirts and sportswear made by his own label, October's Very Own.

MAGIC

'I only rap over a track if it has a magical quality.'

The moody man

Nicki Minaj

Minaj's smash hit single 'Super Bass' catapulted her to fame and sold five million copies in the US alone.

Nicki Minaj has a distinctive rapping style famous for its fast flow and use of different accents. It is no surprise that Lil Wayne knew he had discovered a star when he signed her to his label in 2009. Minaj's first album, *Pink Friday*, featured hits like 'Super Bass' and 'Fly', which is a duet with Rihanna. In just three years she managed to make three albums, three mixtapes and over 60 singles, racking up collaborations with artists like Drake, Ariana Grande, Eminem, The Lonely Island, Mariah Carey, David Guetta, and more.

BUSINESS QUEEN

Like her role model Jay-Z, Minaj is business minded: she launched a perfume named Pink Friday, after her first album, and partnered up with Beats By Dre in 2013 to create her own 'Pink Pill' wireless speaker.

SELECTED DISCOGRAPHY

2008
Sucka Free (mixtape)

2009
We Are Young Money (compilation)

2010
Pink Friday

2012
Pink Friday: Roman Reloaded – The Re-Up

2014
The Pinkprint

SCANDAL

In 2014, Minaj's video for 'Only' provoked anger for its use of graphics and visuals that resembled those of the Nazis – she later apologised.

FEUD

Nicki loves confrontation in her craft and is not afraid to battle it out with fellow rappers. She insulted rappers Remy Ma and Lil' Kim on her 2007 mixtape, and Minaj has also taken shots at pop star Miley Cyrus.

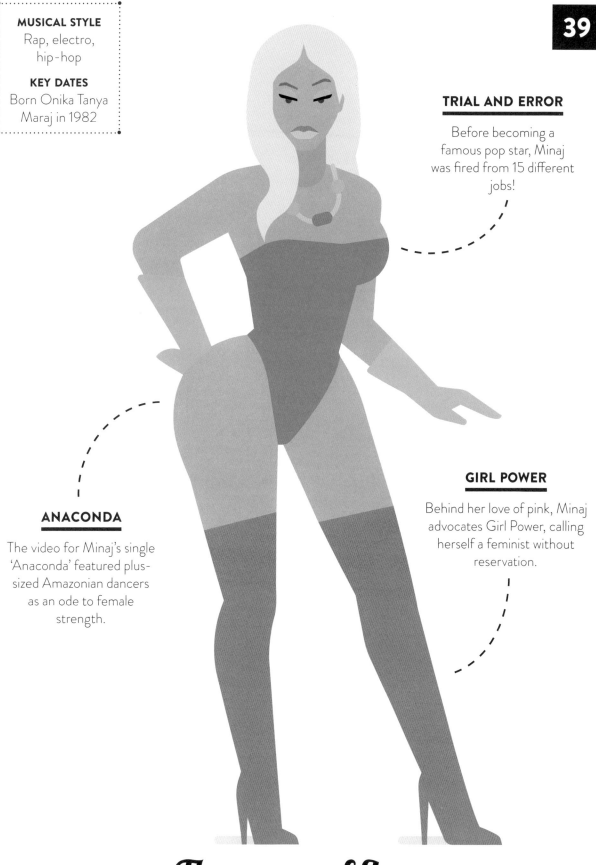

TRIAL AND ERROR

Before becoming a
famous pop star, Minaj
was fired from 15 different
jobs!

ANACONDA

The video for Minaj's single
'Anaconda' featured plus-
sized Amazonian dancers
as an ode to female
strength.

GIRL POWER

Behind her love of pink, Minaj
advocates Girl Power, calling
herself a feminist without
reservation.

The queen of flow

The Weeknd

In 2010, the 20-year-old Canadian Abel Makkonen Tesfaye started posting videos he had recorded in his bedroom onto YouTube under the name 'The Weeknd'. A few years later he was performing at the Grammys. Known for his enigmatic musical style, a cross between R&B, pop and electro, The Weeknd exploded onto the scene in 2015 with the release of his second album, featuring the hit single 'Can't Feel My Face'. His third album saw collaborations with Kendrick Lamar and Daft Punk. The Weeknd is now a worldwide sensation.

INFLUENCES

The Weeknd cites Michael Jackson, David Bowie, Prince, Talking Heads, Wu-Tang Clan, Bad Brains, 50 Cent, Eminem and R. Kelly as inspiration.

GREATEST HIT

'Starboy', his track that features Daft Punk, remained in the UK Top 10 for 15 weeks.

SELECTED DISCOGRAPHY

2011
House of Balloons (mixtape)

2012
Trilogy

2013
Kiss Land

2015
Beauty Behind The Madness

2016
Starboy

FUTURE

In 2017, The Weeknd appeared on 'Comin' Out Strong', a song on the fifth album by Future, the Atlantan rapper, marking the fourth time the pair have sung together.

EMINEM

For one of the remix versions of his single 'The Hills', The Weeknd invited Eminem to his studio to record. Eminem accepted the invitation and the resulting collaboration was an opportunity for the Weeknd to pay homage to his idol.

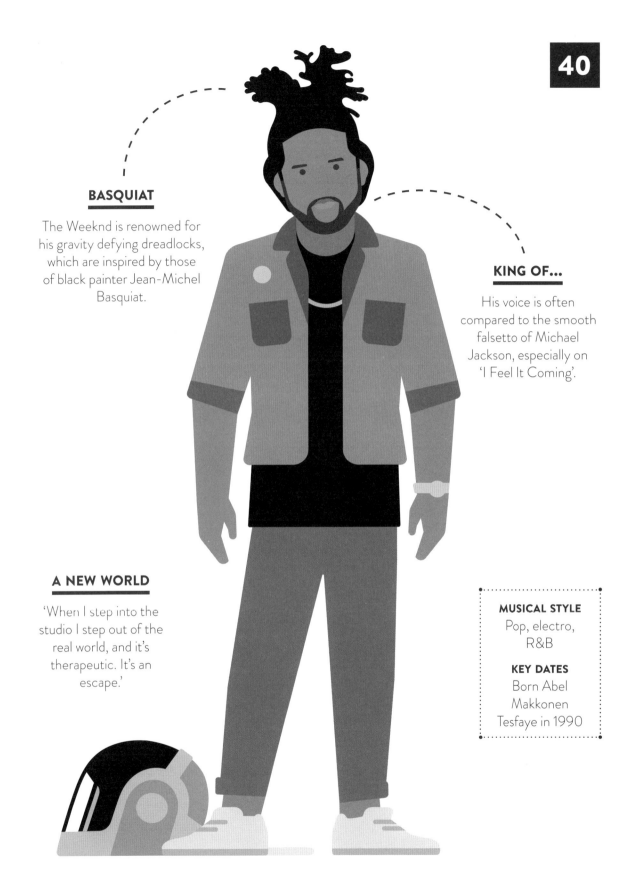

BASQUIAT

The Weeknd is renowned for his gravity defying dreadlocks, which are inspired by those of black painter Jean-Michel Basquiat.

KING OF...

His voice is often compared to the smooth falsetto of Michael Jackson, especially on 'I Feel It Coming'.

A NEW WORLD

'When I step into the studio I step out of the real world, and it's therapeutic. It's an escape.'

MUSICAL STYLE
Pop, electro, R&B

KEY DATES
Born Abel Makkonen Tesfaye in 1990

The new Michael?

Chronology

1936

Robert Johnson records *Sweet Home Chicago*, one of the first examples of the blues – the genre that eventually gives birth to rock.

1969

The **Jackson 5** reach number 1 with their first single 'I Want You Back', led by the 11-year-old Michael.

1981

Stevie Wonder writes 'Happy Birthday', a political song advocating for the birthday of activist Martin Luther King to become a national holiday in the United States.

1988

N.W.A scandalise with their first album, *Straight Outta Compton*, which popularises the Californian rap style known as gangsta rap.

2007

Rihanna releases 'Umbrella' with Jay-Z. The track kickstarts her career and sees her nominated for three Grammys, winning the one for the best collaboration.

2009

On 25 June, **Michael Jackson** dies aged 50. The King of Pop is mourned across the world within a matter of minutes, as news spreads across the internet.

1977

At the height of disco, **Donna Summer** performs 'I Feel Love', produced by Giorgio Moroder, the electro trailblazer.

1979

The Sugarhill Gang release the iconic 'Rapper's Delight', the single that takes rap across the world and spearheads the hip-hop movement.

1996

2Pac, the rapper behind the bestselling 'California Love', is shot at a drive-by in Las Vegas and dies on Friday 13 September.

2003

Missy Elliott released three albums in three years and by 2003 she was confirmed as the bestselling female rapper of all time – she is still the reigning champion.

2011

Beyoncé is the first woman ever to headline Glastonbury music festival on the Pyramid stage.

2012

Drake releases his album *Views*, which is number 1 for 13 weeks in a row and goes platinum in the first week of its release.

Inspiring | Educating | Creating | Entertaining

Brimming with creative inspiration, how-to projects, and useful information to enrich your everyday life, Quarto Knows is a favourite destination for those pursuing their interests and passions. Visit our site and dig deeper with our books into your area of interest: Quarto Creates, Quarto Cooks, Quarto Homes, Quarto Lives, Quarto Drives, Quarto Explores, Quarto Gifts, or Quarto Kids.

Black Music Greats © 2017 Gallimard Jeunesse, Paris
Translation © 2019 Quarto Publishing plc.

First Published in 2017 in French by Gallimard Jeunesse, France.
First Published in 2019 in English by Wide Eyed Editions, an imprint of
The Quarto Group
The Old Brewery, 6 Blundell Street, London N7 9BH, United Kingdom.
T (0)20 7700 6700 F (0)20 7700 8066 **www.QuartoKnows.com**

ISBN 978-1-78603-470-0

The illustrations were created digitally
Set in Brandon Grotesque and Gotham Rounded

Translated by Lili Owen Rowlands
Edited by Lucy Brownridge
Designed by Nicola Price
Production by Nicolas Zeifman

Manufactured in Guangdong, China CC112018
9 8 7 6 5 4 3 2 1

Collect the rest in the series!

Fantastic Footballers
978-1-78603-146-4

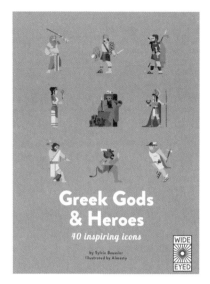

Greek Gods & Heroes
978-1-78603-147-1

Music Legends
978-1-78603-149-5

People of Peace
978-1-78603-148-8

Super Scientists
978-1-78603-473-1